RECALLED TO DEATH

RECALLED TO DEATH

A Martha Gunn Mystery

Priscilla Masters

Severn House Large Print
London & New York

This first large print edition published 2016
in Great Britain and the USA by
SEVERN HOUSE PUBLISHERS LTD of
19 Cedar Road, Sutton, Surrey, England, SM2 5DA.
First world regular print edition published 2015 by
Severn House Publishers Ltd.

British Library Cataloguing in Publication Data
A CIP catalogue record for this title is available from the British Library.

ISBN-13: 9780727894588

Severn House Publishers support the Forest Stewardship Council™
[FSC™], the leading international forest certification organisation. All
our titles that are printed on FSC certified paper carry the FSC logo.

Typeset by Palimpsest Book Production Ltd.,
Falkirk, Stirlingshire, Scotland.
Printed and bound in Great Britain by
T J International, Padstow, Cornwall.

Beware of those who are homeless by choice.

Robert Southey, 1774–1843

Prologue

Umbrella in one hand, flowers in the other, she found it easily enough in the municipal grave-yard, amongst the rows of tombstones, a place put aside for those who had no name. Plot 171, a mound of damp mud, rain trickling over the soil in tiny rivulets the only sign of movement. No flowers, no name. Simply a wooden stake in the ground and the title: Plot 171. His new iden-tity. She almost smiled. For a moment she stood still, struggling to believe that he was really underneath this anonymous pile of earth, then she bunched the stems together and laid the flowers down. Roses, deep, dark red, the colour of love, blood and betrayal, and lilies, white and scented. Funereal.

And dangerous. It was dangerous for her to be here.

A woman, on her knees, tending an adjacent grave, glanced across at her curiously and asked her the same question the sextant had. 'Did you know him then?'

She shook her head. And almost heard the cock crow. Another lie to add to the legion of lies she'd already told. What would one more matter? But somehow, compared to the others, this denial seemed the very worst. To rob him of his identity,

1

to allow him to remain forever unknown, his grave unmarked, his name missing. For ever? Her mouth curved not with a smile but with cynicism, her eyes narrow, feline, cruel. Plot 171. The unknown soldier.

She almost choked. But he was dead now and she could do or say nothing in reparation except give him back the dignity of his identity: his name. His past. She stood a moment longer, thinking.

Phrases ran through her head. The unknown soldier. Known unto God.

She made her decision. That would have to be enough.

She turned and walked away, the phrase ringing in her ears.

Plot 171. Known unto God.

One

Six weeks earlier.
Thursday, 11 September, 9 p.m.

An autumn mist shrouded the ruin, heavy and cold as a sodden grey blanket, the rain dripping over the stones, playing its own wet melody. Splash, tinkle, drip. Splash . . .
  All else was still and cold and quiet, the ruined house wary and watchful as it had learnt to be over the centuries. Watchful but powerless to protect the man who lay in its wrecked embrace.

Thursday, 11 September, 9.15 p.m.
The White House.

Sam was grumpy. He'd been moping around the house all evening while Martha waited for him to get whatever it was off his chest. This was not like her son, who was naturally buoyant and optimistic, not a sulker or a brooder. She eyed him across the table, playing with his supper instead of wolfing it down as he usually did, his gaze downcast, shoulders heaving in heavy, bothered sighs. It was her way to wait for him to speak rather than prompt him, so the silence stretched. His eyes flickered up towards her then away again and she knew he would pick his moment. Eventually he cracked. He gave a few

3

groans as warning, let his fork clatter on to the plate, cleared his throat and looked up.

'Mum,' he said tentatively.

'Sam?'

Another deep sigh. 'I feel stagnant.'

She frowned at the word. This was not what she had been expecting. She looked at her son. Eighteen years old. Signed up with Stoke City FC. Thick, unruly hair with only a touch of her dreadful red. Teeth inclined to be crooked and uneven but lately being forced into line with a brace. He grinned at her scrutiny, his brown eyes soft and affectionate.

'Stagnant?' she queried.

'My mates,' he said in his gruff voice. 'They're all going off to uni. You know – studying stuff. Training for a profession or something anyway. Going off. Leaving home. But me? It's still training four times a week. Matches. Home. Away.' He was bobbing his head at the routine as he spoke. 'Doing the same thing year in, year out.' He looked at her, his brown eyes appealing. 'It isn't enough, Mum. I want to . . .' He looked around him, his eyes searching for something. 'Broaden my horizons,' he said finally, with a touch of bravado. '*Do* something else. *Go* somewhere else. *Be* somewhere else. Be some*one* else.' His eyes were impassioned and sincere and she did not doubt this sincerity.

She gritted her teeth. Somehow she had always expected this – that Sam would, one day, need more than just football in his life. Most people envy the professional whose job is doing what they can only do for fun. But in reality it is like

4

many dreams: the dream becomes a reality and then humdrum. Few ask a professional footballer about the big afterwards. Few say: 'And then what? What do you do when you're dropped from the team? Or injured? Or the new manager dislikes you?' Or ask what happens when they get older. Not everyone can be a Beckham.

Instead, people focus on the glamorous here and now, on the string of noughts that follow what they consider to be a living wage. Sam did make good money. She banked it, invested it and he had access to all he needed. But he was still so young. Still a teenager. He had had driving lessons and bought himself a modest car which relieved her of taxi duty, something she found rather sad. She'd always enjoyed those chats driving him to and from games or training. And at the same time as she'd been relieved of a duty she had rarely found irksome, she gained a new worry – that he would have an accident. Motherhood, she thought as she eyed her son across the kitchen table. It came with a furrowed brow and always something to worry about. So yes, Sam was currently financially independent. But the money he'd made wouldn't last his whole life. And so she constantly did ask the questions: what next? What then? She met his gaze straight on, understanding exactly what he was saying. 'Well,' she said, challenging him, 'Sam Gunn.' She smiled at him, feeling warmth bounce off toffee-brown eyes, so like Martin's. 'If you want to broaden your horizons, how are you going to go about it?'

It had always been her way of parenting to

encourage them to solve their own life's problems with only a little of a push from her. They had hardly known their father so it had been her advice alone. Sam's face twisted in a thoughtful expression while she watched silently. There was a small pattern of faint freckles on his nose that changed shape when he was thinking. She watched them, fascinated. Then he scooped up a deep breath ready to dive from the top diving board. 'I'm going to apply for uni,' he said. 'But not straight away. In a couple of years. I'll stay with Stoke for a bit longer. I'm going to save up some money to see me through uni.' He grinned, showing his brace off to perfection, 'So I don't have to depend on you. I'm going to study for A-levels and I'm going to talk to the manager. He's got a mate who gives career advice, sort of.'

She interrupted him. 'And you trust them?'

'Yeah,' he said seriously. 'I do. I'm going to talk to them and discuss my future. Football won't last for ever, Mum.'.

'No,' she agreed. 'It won't. And I know it's difficult with your friends going off to uni. What about Tom?'

Tom Dempsey was Sam's best friend.

'He thinks the same as I do.'

'Good.'

Sam scooped in another deep breath. 'So, next year, I'm going to re-sit my A-levels.' His expression was now watchful, waiting for her response, which was an encouraging smile.

'And then what?'

'I want to be a teacher,' he said simply, his

expression faintly anxious, as though she would not think this a worthy ambition.

She nodded. She had expected that at some point he would look beyond the beautiful game, but this was a surprise to her. Somehow she had not guessed at teaching. It would take some getting used to.

Sam grinned at her. 'At least with my football money I won't have to have a student loan. Will I?'

She simply laughed.

Thursday, 11 September, 9.30 p.m.

Detective Inspector Alex Randall watched the vehicle leave his home with the usual sense of hopelessness, anger, frustration and concern. They would take her. Again. They would patch her up. Again. And then she would come home *again* and the whole sorry circus would start up all over again. He turned away from the blue light strobing down the road, neighbours no doubt watching from behind their twitching curtains. Chatter clatter. Idle chatter and speculation. He felt despair. He was so tired of this. He wanted another life. He turned away and closed the front door behind him.

Two

Friday, 12 September, 10.30 a.m.

John Hyde, his name was. An English name and it suited him well. He was stolid, reliable and honest. Bouncy and energetic. English Heritage paid him to open the gates of Moreton Corbet Castle at 10.30 a.m. during the week, so that was exactly what he did. On the dot. In his early sixties, having taken early retirement from an accountancy firm, he had been hoping to slide into retirement: gardening, an allotment and Viking River Cruises with his wife, Margaret. But Margaret had died unexpectedly of a particularly voracious form of leukaemia, leaving him with no one to cruise or garden with. It had not gone according to plan. But John Hyde was a stoic and, as he was fond of repeating to his friends at the golf club, he didn't do, 'sorry for myself'. He was making a determined effort to 'fill my time' and this was one of the ways he did it, by acting as custodian to the dramatically beautiful but ruined facade of Moreton Corbet Castle, which always reminded him of a very beautiful woman with a terrible facial injury like Holmes's Veiled Lodger.

The odd fact about Moreton Corbet Castle was that it had never been anything but a ruin. There had been a house there which was damaged

8

during the Civil War and a rebuild. But it was never completed, due, some said, to a curse from a man named Paul Homlyard, who had obviously had supernatural talents.

After the rain of last night it was a bright, golden morning, and Hyde filled his lungs with the pure country air. He unlocked the padlock of the small gate and, not for the first time, as he strode across the field towards the ruin he looked up at the dramatic facade which he had photographed on numerous occasions: in fresh spring, snowy winter, summer's heat haze and autumn's colours. It always looked beautiful and this morning especially so. He felt his spirits soar. It was an amazing place. The windows, glassless, blinded by war and superstition. He felt a frisson of excitement. The jagged edges of the stones which contrasted with the smooth elegance of the Queen Ann facade. A facade which, in spite of its ruined state, still stood tall and shapely against the bluest of skies promising such a wonderful interior – yet inside it was disappointing. There was *no* interior, only piles of tumbled stones and mown grass. But like many people, Hyde was perfectly aware that sometimes hints and promises, expectations and imagination were more exciting than reality could ever be. The retirement he had planned with Margaret may well have settled into the humdrum and not been the endless rounds of golf, cruises and gardening in a perfect weather balance of sunshine and light showers, but cold and dreary with periods of mind-numbing boredom. So he accepted the limitations of the house which hinted at its dramatic and haunted past.

It was his custom to wander around the perimeter of the grounds and then inspect the stonework, checking that all was well, making sure there was no litter, no discarded lager cans or, horror of horrors, pizza boxes. They were his pet hate. He couldn't believe how people would simply discard their detritus and leave this lovely place a mess. But there you were, he chuntered as he marched around the area. People were people. And English Heritage didn't secure the premises all that well because there was nothing of value here. It was simply a ruin. There was nothing to guard, nothing to steal. So the only security was the padlocked gate which anybody could vault over.

Today he felt his spirits lift. The sun was golden; there were no Styrofoam food containers, no lager cans and no pizza boxes. Not even a biodegradable apple core. All was neat and tidy, quiet and organized. The grounds were a rich green, still damp and freshly mown, the signs clean and undefaced. He walked inside the remains of the dining chamber, in the shadow now of the tall walls, the sun momentarily blocked out. He crossed to the far end of the room, to the lower chamber, and peered down the steps into the vaulted stone cellar.

And instantly knew: something was wrong. It took him a few minutes to work out what it was. An iron railing protected the area, and beyond that there was a short flight of shallow stone steps. He glanced down. There was a splash of rust on the third step down which looked like paint. But it wasn't rust and it wasn't paint either. He knew exactly what it was. He removed the railing and descended the steps with grim apprehension. There was a smell too. A butcher's shop smell. Rich and sweet but also frightening. It was the sweet stench of blood. He peered into the gloom and immediately spotted something in the corner. A huddle of blankets or a coat or . . .

He was still frowning as he went over to touch it and realized it was not just a coat: someone was wearing it. He jerked back. 'Hello?' he said, startled. The person did not move; neither did he answer. Hyde fished a flashlight from his pocket and shone it into the man's face. The man stared up at him, glassy eyed, skin ghost white, two weeks' stubble. At first he thought that a scarlet scarf was tied around his throat. Hyde peered closer then stood for a moment, unable to take in what he was seeing and unable also to move, act or even vocalize. He was glued to the spot, the glue seeping into his throat too. He couldn't scream or shout. He simply gagged and was stuck to the floor. His eyes were fixed on the gaping wound beneath the man's chin, moving only briefly to take in the eyes – glazed, almost closed. But he must have stretched out a hand and touched him because the man's skin, he remembered later, had felt fish-cold.

He stood for a moment, paralysed, then shook himself and moistened his throat. 'Get a grip, Hyde,' he exhorted himself hoarsely, his voice sounding loud with a wavering echo as it bounced around the small chamber with its domed ceiling.

11

Then a wave of terror rippled right through him as a new thought struck. Someone had done this. He looked back up the steps, at the arc of light at the top, suddenly fearful. This man had not inflicted that horrible wound on himself. He noticed no knife. He took a step back. Was a killer out there, at the top of the steps, waiting for him? Was he hidden behind the jagged stones, watching and waiting for him to find . . . this? His head swivelled back. Was he waiting for him to emerge from this . . . tomb?

John backed up the steps, his ears straining for any sound, his eyes moving from the person in the corner to the exterior which both beckoned and threatened. He was now searingly aware of his own real terror, his eyes peering around. When he reached the top he looked across the tumbled stones, so familiar and now so strange. He walked quickly back through the archway which lacked a door, constantly scanning the ruin, imagining he felt a cold finger or a sharp blade stroke his own throat, his panicked ears full of a rushing sound as loud as a waterfall as he strained to hear: a loose stone falling, a quiet step across the grass, the sound of another's breathing. Was the person who had done this still here? Were they now waiting for him? In this dead house there were secret passages and rooms partially blocked by stones. There were plenty of places for a killer to hide. His eyes darted around the site but they could not see everywhere. They couldn't peer into priests' holes or search secret passages. And this was a deceitful house which was not as it seemed. The facade made a great pretence at past splendour but in reality it never had been the complete great house it masqueraded as. War and superstition had put paid to that. Someone could easily still be hiding here, watching him from behind the stones, peering through the fallen archways, stalking him, waiting for him to find the dead man.

His walk broke into a run back towards the gate, still mercifully open. His eyes skittered from one tumbled wall to another. Children who came here to play hide and seek were not always found quickly. Its angles and random passages were perfect for hiding or playing dead in. He looked back towards the lower chamber. The man was not playing dead. And now John Hyde had reached the relative safety of the gate. His eyes scanned the ragged ramparts and his ears registered only stillness. Apart from a blackbird's liquid song there was no sight or sound of anyone. And now he was a little calmer he recalled something. When he had arrived at the small car park it had been empty. And now he was out in the open again he almost wondered whether he had imagined the entire incident – the dead man slumped against the wall, the wound across his throat, the spots of blood on the steps and the smell . . .

He closed his eyes, but that brought the picture all too vividly back, with more detail. The man with the terrible wound, hands flung back, the thick coat he had been wearing drenched with blood, the rusty sprays across the walls and ceiling which told their own story. And more: the man's grey, shocked complexion, the grubby trousers, his legs outstretched and he remembered something else. Clinging around the dead man, polluting the small cellar had been another scent – the smell of staleness, the smell of the unwashed, the homeless. Only then did Hyde fumble in his pocket for his mobile phone.

The fingers that pressed the three digits were shaking.

Three

At Monkmoor police station in Shrewsbury, DI Randall was struggling to appear normal and professional when inside all was turmoil. He was sitting, motionless, at his desk. Something inside him was bubbling up and he wasn't quite sure how to deal with it. He knew he'd had enough. He knew he couldn't carry on like this. He recognized he had come to the end of his tether. But what was he going to do with her? Erica? He slammed his hand down on the desk then dropped his head down, defeated. Whichever way he looked at the situation, it crushed him. He could not see any way through. Every solution brought more problems in its wake. Each problem compounded the other like Hydra's head and there was no way he could have what he wanted. Randall's mouth twisted in a smile. His heart's desire.

Then he sat up straight. 'Not going to happen, Alex,' he murmured. 'Just not going to happen. There is nothing you can do except accept and live with *the situation*.'

The knock on the door was a welcome distraction.

'Sir.' Even more so when it was Detective Sergeant Paul Talith's plump, happy face which peered round.

15

'Talith?'

'Body's been found at Moreton Corbet, sir.'

Randall raised his eyebrows. Moreton Corbet was a spectacular ruin eight miles to the north-east of Shrewsbury, near the RAF base at Shawbury. Some might describe it as a house that had never been finished. Others as a house with a past. One thing was for sure: it had a bad history. And now this.

Talith continued, frowning, an expression of disgust darkening his features, 'According to the member of the public who found him it looks like his throat's been cut, sir.'

Randall looked up, his troubles dissolving like sugar in boiling water. He was suddenly aware, given this sense of perspective, that his own problems were small, practically non-existent. 'Is anyone out there?'

'Gethin Roberts, sir.'

Randall smothered a smile. Roberts was a PC who frequently found himself in the thick of it. He'd seen a body washed out from a cellar, tried to save a boy from a burning house, recovered the body of a suicide from a police cell, held a long-dead baby. And Roberts would glance around, bemused at where he found himself. Then he would embellish and exaggerate to his long-suffering, long-time partner, Flora Connelly. Detective Inspector Alex Randall knew a lot more about his officers than they realized.

He was already on his feet and reaching for his jacket. 'Let's go and rescue Roberts then, shall we?'

* * *

A few miles away (left turn at Shawbury), PC Gethin Roberts, summoned by the 999 team as the officer nearest to the call, had pulled up in the squad car, leaving the blue light flashing almost as reassurance as well as a signal. The law was here. Hyde strode towards him, meeting him on the road. He was a big man, a little pale from his recent experience but with a strong tread and a steady gaze, and he had recovered himself enough to proffer a firm handshake.

Roberts introduced himself and Hyde ventured a traumatized smile.

'You have no idea how glad I am to see you,' he confessed. 'There's something beyond scary about being here alone with a murdered man.' He couldn't resist scanning the area, as if still half expecting to see a madman brandishing a knife come screaming, like Braveheart, towards him.

Roberts began to say something about not being certain the man had been murdered. Hyde responded with a 'Harrumph' and 'his throat's been cut.'

Roberts gulped. *Why was it always him? Why was he always first on the scene?*

'Besides,' Hyde continued eagerly, 'I didn't see a weapon. And wouldn't he still have been grasping it?'

Roberts nodded noncommittally. He wasn't absolutely sure about this but he thought prob-ably . . . yes.

Roberts took down Hyde's details and followed him through the small gate which he immediately sealed off with *Do Not Cross* tape. They headed towards the shell of a house.

In spite of his apprehension, Roberts couldn't resist being impressed by the ruin. 'Gosh,' he said, looking up at the three-storeyed Queen Anne facade. 'What a place. How long's it been like this?'

Hyde turned around, humour on his lips and in his eyes. 'Oh, about four hundred years,' he said casually.

Roberts gaped at him. 'Really?'

Hyde smothered a smile. 'Yes, really,' he said.

For the briefest of moments the body was forgotten in awe and respect for the building. Then Roberts cleared his throat. 'Hmm,' he said, trying to sound authoritative. 'You'd better take me to . . .' He felt sick. It was about the last thing he wanted to do – view a body with a cut throat. But he was a police officer.

'Yes, of course.' Hyde immediately returned to the grave matter. 'Sorry.'

As they walked, Roberts started his questions. 'What time did you discover the body?'

'It would have been just after 10.30 a.m.,' Hyde said. 'I always take a look around the site first. Check it, you know, for any vandalism or rubbish. That sort of thing.'

They had reached the Great Tower. As though it was a learned line, Hyde could not resist muttering, 'Built in 1200 AD.'

PC Gethin Roberts nodded.

A long time ago then. They climbed over a pile of stones and walked into a long, oblong area.

'This is the dining chamber,' Hyde supplied, then climbed through what might once have been a window and headed towards some stone steps. 'Down here,' he said.

Roberts followed him, dread slowing his step and making his feet heavy.

The cellar was brick lined, with a low domed ceiling. Roberts, six foot two inches, needed to duck to enter it. The light was gloomy as the entrance faced east and the light was blocked by a tumbled wall outside. It was chilly and dank, the usual scent of stale air and urine. People will use anywhere as a piss pot, Roberts thought. He took another step down, saw the stains on the step and registered the new smell. He had brought out his flashlight and illuminated the huddle in the corner. Hyde stuck close behind him.

Handing the torch to Hyde, Roberts slipped on a pair of latex gloves and bent over the man. Hyde directed the beam on the wound but averted his eyes away from the figure. Roberts took it all in: the position of the body, still propped up in the corner, supported by the stone, the thick coat open, the wound a bright scarf around his neck, his anatomy all too visible. And blood? He looked around him. It was everywhere. It had sprayed out in an arc, defacing the wall and ceiling, and a large pool of it was on the man's clothing, down the front of his sweater, soaking into his coat and the ground at his feet. Roberts felt suddenly claustrophobic in this dank cellar, his exit blocked by Hyde. To counteract the feeling, Roberts performed his usual defence, silently recanting lectures on the preservation of evidence at crime scenes.

Keep your eyes open and be aware where your feet are treading.

He took a step forward, the phrases swimming around his head like a random shoal of herring changing direction, flicking here, flicking there. *Isolate the scene. Preserve the evidence. Avoid contamination.* That was the first rule. He frowned. Oh, no, it wasn't. The first rule was: *Make sure your victim really is dead.*

'Not a lot of doubt about that, boyo,' he muttered to himself. Then he remembered a salient point from a particularly cynical lecturer in forensic psychology and swivelled his head to peer back at the person who was blocking his exit. *And don't forget: the person who finds the body is often the last person to have seen the person alive. No, really,* the lecturer had insisted when another junior constable had demurred. *You'd be surprised how many killers want to be the one to make the headlines, live the drama, report the crime and gauge the police responses without acknowledging their part in it. They want to involve themselves.*

Roberts eyed the man suspiciously.

The lecturer had pursued the point. *Keep an open mind.*

He would certainly do that. He focused back on his victim.

He didn't need to move the coat to see the white face, the mouth open in a grimace and glazed eyes peering at him from beneath drooped lids. Or to register the blood staining, or the gaping wound in the throat. Wet hair, long and unkempt, was stuck to the scalp. Roberts sniffed

20

the air and breathed in the very same smell that Hyde had earlier: sweet blood and underneath that, the stale smell of the unwashed. He looked closer at the man's thick tweed coat. It was filthy. Roberts thought then: thank God it was too chilly for flies. They were Roberts's particular hate ever since he had witnessed a flyblown body washed out of a cellar when the Severn River had flooded. He reached out a hand, hoping that Mr Hyde would not see he was trembling like a blanc-mange, and stupidly touched the man while at the same time recalling the lecturer's advice: *Use your eyes, not your hands.*

So Roberts looked around him. There was blood on the floor around the man and plenty on his coat too. He took the torch from Hyde, who was standing over him with a fixed smile. Roberts flashed the torch on the ceiling and saw the spray of blood. He touched the front of the coat. The blood was stiff. First on the scene, Roberts, he thought, again. And now he started to make deductions. The man had been killed here. This was the crime scene. Time to call in the reinforcements. He went over the process.

Call for reinforcements. Summon the police surgeon. Bag up the hands. Tape off an access route. Above all: preserve the evidence. And take a statement from your witness, bearing in mind he just could be your perpetrator.

But first of all . . . He looked up at the short flight of steps and, hoping his witness wouldn't realize his motive was to escape the cellar and avoid being sick, suggested they move upstairs.

He immediately felt better in the relatively

21

fresh, clean air and focused on Hyde, hoping he wouldn't realize he was being interrogated. 'When were you last here – before this morning, I mean?'

Hyde looked worried. 'It isn't open every day,' he said defensively, 'but I take a quick shifty around most mornings.'

'Did you yesterday morning?'

Hyde frowned, as though anxious to give the exact truth. 'Yes,' he said. 'I was here around nine, I think.'

Roberts glanced back down the steps. 'I take it he . . .' his eyes signalled down towards the top of the cellar steps, '. . . wasn't here then?'

'Of course not.' Hyde was affronted.

Roberts took a look around him. 'I don't think you'll be opening to the public for a while yet,' he added. 'We're going to have to shut off the site.'

Hyde made no response to this.

That was when the reinforcements turned up.

Four

Roberts was getting fidgety. The troops were here but there still seemed to be an inordinate wait for anything to happen. There was a long wait at the gate while the car park, no more than a lay-by really, was sealed off in case there were tyre marks. A plan of action was formulated, the approaches to the crime scene clearly marked out. Then there was the wait for the forensic team to assemble and another wait for the arc lights to arrive and a tent to be erected around the entrance to the cellar to shield forensic activities from public view. Then there was yet another long wait for the police surgeon and/or the forensic pathologist to make a formal pronouncement of death. And a wait for the photographer to record everything before they could touch a thing. He knew the theory but it didn't diminish his impatience with the system. Once the body is moved you have disturbed the crime scene for ever, perhaps destroying the one piece of evidence which would have led you to the killer. Then there was a wait for the SOCO team to start analysing the crime scene. A wait for the coroner to give permission to move the body to the mortuary for the post-mortem. A wait for equipment to

23

arrive. A van to use as an operational base. A wait for . . .

And all the time in the background the investigation would be beginning, officers taking statements, asking questions, finding out who saw what. And if possible find out who the poor blighter is – or was.

Roberts fidgeted, impatient to be moving.

DI Alex Randall was a little more brisk. Almost as soon as he arrived, he donned a forensic suit and approached the remains of the castle. Even with the job in hand, he couldn't resist admiring the skyline before approaching the cellar. It took him less than five minutes to make a preliminary assessment. 'Do we know who he is?'

Roberts shook his head. 'I've had a quick look through his coat pockets, sir,' he said. 'Just bits and pieces.'

Randall looked up. 'No wallet? No driving licence? No ID at all?'

PC Gethin Roberts shook his head. 'I've only looked through his coat pockets, sir,' he said, flushing slightly. He didn't want to confess that opening the buttons and touching the smelly old sweater had made him almost as sick as the thought of the congealed blood and the throat wound.

Randall frowned. 'Any sign of a weapon?'

'Not so far, sir.'

Randall's frown deepened. The victim looked and smelt a vagrant. His clothes were filthy, as were his fingernails, and there was a few weeks' stubble on his chin. Last night had been rainy. Possibly if he was homeless he'd decided to

24

shelter here for the night and . . . had somehow met his fate. Randall looked around him. The blood spatter told its own story.

Judging by the position of the body the sequence of events had been this: the man had been down here, and someone had come down the steps. The man had stood up. The perpetrator had slashed at his throat – Randall's eyes swivelled upwards to a telling spray of blood on the ceiling – and the man had stumbled backwards into the corner, dying more or less instantly. One could almost picture the action. Here . . . a spray of blood which had diminished as the man had fallen backwards.

Randall studied the hands Roberts had already bagged up separately. There was blood on them. He had clutched at his throat and staggered backwards. Randall took a quick look around the cellar. There didn't appear to be anything else here. It didn't look like the tramp had made himself a bed. Possibly he had simply relied on his thick coat as his mattress, pillow and blankets. Last night had been rainy rather than cold. Randall ascended the steps thoughtfully, already piecing events together in his mind. There wasn't a lot else he could do until the pathologist arrived. He and Talith made a survey of the site, which consisted of a large grassy area surrounded by the ruins of a tower, gatehouse, halls and a dining chamber.

What had brought the man here? he wondered. The area wasn't exactly popular, except with historians and on summer afternoons when families would picnic here. Out of hours few people

25

would venture here by chance, particularly on a wet September evening. Courting couples, maybe. But would a courting couple slit the throat of a peeping Tom? The man had been concealed in the cellar, not chased there. Had he been chased there surely he would have been stabbed in the back, not had his throat cut . . . unless he had turned to face his attacker. So had the man come here purely by chance? Had the murder also been by chance? Who would want to slit the throat of a vagrant? Why? And why here? This was a small, rural hamlet – a church, a farmhouse, a few pretty cottages. Why had this man come here in the first place? Shelter? Had he come here deliberately? Had there been an assignation? Had someone lured him here? There was, of course, another possibility. What if there had been a drug deal which their dead man had stumbled across? Randall scratched his head, frowning. To his knowledge this was not a known place for drug swaps. But there was a first time for everything. Was there any significance in the fact that his body had been found here, in these particular ruins? Who was he? How had he got here?

Wandering around, he studied the environs. Moreton Corbet Castle was in an area roughly the size of a field. It was reached via a small gate thickly hedged from the road. To the west was farmland. Cattle were currently grazing there. To the east was a church and a pretty cottage which had once been the vicarage. The site itself was interesting, particularly to historians. There was a twelfth-century tower, a sixteenth-century kitchen and garderobe and a late sixteenth-century dining chamber. The cellar was on the south side of this, reached over a small mound.

The Elizabethan facade had come later but was never finished, and by the eighteenth century Moreton Corbet Castle was nothing but a ruin, as it was today.

Randall's mind started working, trying to track back and work out the events leading to this murder. And as usual he started by making lists, planning the action and allocations of suitable officers. First port of call was to speak to the person who lived in the cottage. Then the farmer who lived in that wonderful black-and-white house opposite. He returned to the cellar, where lights had been set up, and studied the dead man's face in more detail. He looked to be somewhere in his late forties/early fifties. It was hard to judge when the wound and death had distorted his features but his hair, though long and uncombed, was dark with only streaks of grey, and he was unkempt. Randall frowned. If he had been a vagrant, there were places for the homeless in Shrewsbury, rooms available where they could have a hot meal, a wash – even use as an address when applying for a job. But there was never enough help and support. Besides, many of the homeless didn't want help. They liked the anonymity the life of a vagrant gave them. They didn't want an identity. They wanted to escape. Well, this one hadn't. Many of the homeless in the town camped in the meadows which bordered the river. Silks Meadow or Frankwell, which was not only prone to flooding but also had a dark history of furtive crime, footpads and smuggling.

Cut throats. Randall was thoughtful. The phrase had stuck in his mind. *Cut throats.*

Some of the homeless were drug addicts; others had mental disorders and some of them . . . well. They just didn't want an average life, wife, home, mortgage, two-point-four children. Randall gave a wry smile. Come to that, neither did he. He wondered if this unidentified man fitted in to this category. Could he be an escapee, or a fugitive?

A lot of the homeless ended up sitting out the night not in shop doorways or under bridges but underneath the comfortable, warm, golden double arch of McDonald's, where the staff sometimes gave them free chips and a hot drink. Not exactly the usual clichéd image of a fast food company. In general, the homeless in Shrewsbury caused few problems. They tended to keep themselves to themselves. Sometimes they were bothered by drunks or drug addicts or simply the general public who resented their state, but mostly the vagrants shuffled around the town ignored and ignoring people themselves. They neither caused bother, nor attracted it.

He turned away from the man and ascended the steps, back out into the welcome light and fresh air, gazed back towards the gate and wondered as he watched the English Heritage gatekeeper. As always, he had to consider all options and, like Roberts, his thoughts settled on Hyde. Now that his initial shock at discovering the crime had abated, his impression was that the caretaker was affronted at the intrusion. It was as though this place was his own personal possession. Randall had seen this phenomenon for himself when visiting stately homes. The people who worked there appeared to feel a personal responsibility and protectiveness towards their charges, not only for the people but also towards the property itself. It was natural that Hyde would resent someone, particularly someone like their victim, trespassing on the property he appeared to think of as his own. He would have taken it as an insult, an affront to the ruined mansion's dignity that this person should doss out in its grounds.

Randall looked at the upright, bearing and uncompromising features of the caretaker. He might be a little rigid, but was it really possible that he would resent a vagrant's intrusion that much? Enough to cut his throat? Surely not. But then Randall decided that this was the point from where they would begin their investigation, with the caretaker of Moreton Corbet Castle.

Hyde gazed back at him. Pale but resolute, saying nothing but very wary.

'OK,' Randall said to Talith, who had been watching him, waiting for him to start directing the operations. 'It is fairly obviously a suspicious death so we set the wheels in motion.'

Gethin Roberts was startled into action and activity.

Randall decided to summon Dr Mark Sullivan, Home Office pathologist, to the scene rather than the police surgeon. Delyth Fontaine was good enough at her job but this was a case for the pathologist. The trouble was it meant further delay. Mark Sullivan was currently at the hospital mortuary performing a post-mortem on a patient who had died while under surgery, so they had to wait for him to arrive. It was an ironic fact that a body, however patently dead it was, could not be moved until a medical practitioner had certified death.

And he had to inform the coroner.

Leaving Talith to organize a forensic van, he pulled out his mobile phone and connected, spoke briefly to Jericho and was put straight through to Martha. It took him just minutes to describe the scene and she authorised the removal of the body once the appropriate certification had been completed. 'When you're ready, Alex,' she said pleasantly.

'It looks like a random killing,' Alex said, 'and the man appears to be a vagrant.'

'A tramp?'

'Yes. It looks like it.'

'Have you had any other assaults on vagrants in this area?'

In spite of the circumstances, Randall smiled. He was used to Martha's curiosity into the police perspective. 'No.'

'So this is an isolated assault – a vicious one.'

'It would appear so,' he said cautiously. 'I certainly hope so.' He paused. 'I only hope this isn't going to be the start of attacks on the homeless but I can't think of a reason why anyone would target a tramp unless they held a grudge against him personally rather than resenting them collectively. Other attacks on the homeless in other areas have proved to be random. But this will, of course, make our job harder.'

'You're not giving up before you start, are you, Alex?' she teased.

He took it in good spirit. 'No, I'm not, but I can foresee problems.'

'I suppose you'll try to find out what his background is and why he took the path into homelessness.'

'It's usually drink or drugs.'

'Or mental illness.'

On the other end of the line, unseen by the coroner, Alex Randall winced as, oblivious, Martha continued, 'Do you think . . . is it possible the reasons behind his vagrancy might be the reason he was killed?'

'You mean someone who had a grudge against people with drink or drug problems or someone with a mental illness?'

'Well, ye-es.'

'It's possible.'

'Or else someone who knew him. Someone who was related to his previous life.'

'In which case he would be a specific target, but I've learned not to be too optimistic. My fear is that our man simply happened to be in the wrong place at the wrong time.'

'When there was a marauding homicidal throat-cutting maniac on the loose?'

Alex chuckled. 'Something like that. Anyway.' He hid behind the usual statements. 'We'll be considering all options and I promise, Martha, to keep you informed and well up to date.'

Martha couldn't resist a chuckle. She knew that the detective was well aware of her interest in crime, of her feeling of responsibility towards

31

justice for those who had died violently, that she felt as though she was both their representative and mouthpiece.

There was a pause while Martha pictured the scene herself. She knew Moreton Corbet Castle well. She'd taken the children there on picnics many times. Like other children, Sam and Sukey had played Roundheads and Cavaliers in and out of the ruins, re-enacting its violent and troubled past. Or else they had pretended to be the castle's ghost, modelling their role on Paul Homlyard, who had cursed the castle when evicted by Vincent Corbet on account of his Puritan beliefs. In order to prolong the game she had spent hours delaying her discovery of the twins amongst the ruins, rounding the tumbled walls, searching in and out of the nooks and crannies in the Great Tower, finally finding them hiding in the fireplace of the dining chamber or down the steps in the cellar, so she could visualize the scene of the murder only too well – the huddled body of a murdered vagrant hidden just there where her own precious kids had watched and chuckled and waited for her to find them. Typical twins, they had always hidden together. And though she was a coroner and dealt in the business of death, Martha Gunn had a particular horror of death by a cut throat. Murder was barbaric enough, but throat cutting seemed particularly so. She realized then that Alex Randall was still on the other end of the line. She had expected him to ring off, but he hadn't. He had waited, kept the line open.

'Alex,' she prompted.

'Martha.' There seemed to be an appeal in his voice.

'Alex?' she said again.

'I – this is an imposition.'

She decided to take the bull by the horns then. Lead him onwards. 'Look, Alex,' she said. 'We're friends. If you want to talk to me about something unrelated to our work together that's perfectly OK with me. Understand?'

He exhaled. 'It's still an imposition.'

'Nonsense,' she said briskly. 'My ears are open. I mean it sincerely. You want to talk? I'm happy to listen.'

His response was a humble, 'Thank you.'

'OK. Now keep me up to date with your case.'

'Yeah. We'll be starting with the usual haunts of the homeless and the people of Moreton Corbet. See if any of them saw anything.'

'OK,' Martha said. 'Keep in touch. And Alex,' she added, 'remember what I said. If you want to offload something my ears are open and attuned. Understand?'

Somehow she knew that the detective was smiling as he put the phone down.

Leaving PC Sean Dart to take down Hyde's details, Randall returned to the cellar, lit now by brilliant arc lights mercilessly illuminating each rounded corner. An access corridor had been searched, cleared of evidence and marked out with tape. It wasn't a large area, no more than eight by eight feet. The spots on the steps were ringed with chalk. The sprays on the ceiling had small markers indicating them and detailed photographs had been taken of the spray pattern. Randall knew enough about forensic science to recognize the fan of droplets as being the result of an artery being severed. Arteries spurt, veins ooze. Blood is under pressure in an artery and spurts with great force if that artery is severed. If the perpetrator had been facing their man at the time of the assault he would have been covered in blood. If, however, he had come up behind him, he would not. But Randall was working on the assumption that the assault had been from a frontal position. He thought it through again. It looked as though their man had come to the bottom of the steps to see who was there and, after the assault, had staggered backwards against the wall and collapsed in the corner. Where their man was still sitting, there was a significant pool of blood. So . . . the questions were still unanswered. Had he come here last night, out of the rain, and been followed or accidentally stumbled upon?

The alternative was that their man had come here to meet someone. The use of a weapon would appear to support this theory. Unless their man had been murdered with his own weapon and the assailant had merely used it against him and taken it away with him.

Suddenly feeling that something wasn't quite right, Randall looked around him. What was it?

Then he knew what it was. All vagrants have belongings. Usually a rucksack full of oddments that never leaves their side: tobacco, warmer clothing, a blanket, something waterproof – bin liner or mac. Where was this guy's? Also, how

34

had he got here? Shrewsbury was eight miles away. There was no bicycle outside. Had he walked all this way? Hitch-hiked? Last night had been cold and rainy but the man's thick tweed coat had been bone dry. Not even a hint of damp. So how long had he been here? When did he come here? When did he die?

As the incident van was manoeuvring into place and Talith was putting up signs, informing the public that Moreton Corbet Castle would be closed to visitors until further notice, Mark Sullivan, the Home Office pathologist, turned up in his black Mercedes. Randall went to meet him.

Five

In the past, Doctor Mark Sullivan, though a skilled Home Office pathologist, had had a drink problem. Both Martha and Alex Randall had noted his hands shaking on more than one occasion and worried about his future. One slip could mean the end of his career. But a year ago he had announced his divorce and this appeared to have resolved the problem. Since then he had gained in both competence and confidence and was much happier. Alex liked working with him and trusted his judgement. If not close friends, the two men were respectful, friendly colleagues.

Having finished his work at the hospital, Sullivan had driven out to Moreton Corbet, enjoying the ride out of the town and the break from the mortuary. He pulled up behind the squad cars and the huge white incident van and donned his forensic suit, gloves and cap included. Then he pushed open the small gate and threaded his way along the narrow marked corridor towards DI Randall, giving him a warm smile. 'So what have you got for me this time, Alex?' He sounded jaunty.

'Looks like a tramp with his throat cut. Poor guy.' He couldn't resist adding, 'Some people have all the luck.'

36

Mark Sullivan grinned. 'Sure it's not one of the local cottagers in their old gardening clothes having an accident with his hedge clippers?'

Randall gave a token smirk. 'Well, whoever he is hopefully we'll soon find out.'

'No ID on him?'

Randall shook his head. 'No. We haven't done a proper search, though. Thought we'd leave that to you.'

Sullivan's good humour was undented. 'Thank you.'

Randall made an attempt at a joke. 'Looks like we have Mr Nobody in there.'

'Who came . . .' Sullivan scanned the grand facade, 'to this impressive place and got his throat cut. Well, if you're going to be killed it may as well be in such a place. Lead on.'

Alex Randall picked his way along the corridor of access, the pathologist practically stepping in his footsteps. They lifted the side of the white tent and entered.

Sullivan was thorough in his approach. He was taking it all in as he entered the lower chamber and approached the steps that led to the cellar. He noted the spots of blood and looked up as though he knew what he was expecting to see – arcs of spray on the ceiling. He approached the corner of the cellar and hunkered down so his face was on the same level as their victim. Saying nothing, he spent a moment or two simply observing the dead man, studying the way he was propped up against the wall, looking at the pools of dried blood that stained his clothing. Then he reached out and touched the man's neck, gloved fingers probing the neck wound quite gently. He examined both the man's wrists and tried to flex his elbow. Even Randall could tell it was stiff.

Sullivan spoke in a soft voice, as though to tag it to himself. 'Rigor mortis is well established.'

He spent more than half an hour making notes and taking photographs of his own. He took the man's axillary temperature and then an ambient reading in the cellar, making as little disturbance of the clothes as possible before he finally stood up. 'Not a lot of doubt about the cause of death, Alex,' he said. 'Throat cut.' He made a face as he glanced back. 'Quite an anatomy lesson. As you can see . . .'

Alex Randall held his hands up. 'OK, Mark,' he said. 'I get the picture. No need for gory detail. Any idea of . . .'

Mark Sullivan cut him short. 'Time of death,' he said, anticipating the detective's question, 'will have been about eighteen hours ago. Give or take six hours.'

Randall thought for a moment. 'So probably sometime yesterday evening – between five and eleven p.m.?'

'Roughly. Somewhere round there, anyway.' He had the pathologists' reluctance for being too precise about the time of death. He turned around, started to peel off his gloves and remove his cap, chucking them into the basket. 'We'd better get the poor fellow to the mortuary and do a proper job.'

'Age?'

Sullivan glanced back at the man. 'Oh, I'd say

somewhere between forty and fifty, wouldn't you agree?'

Randall nodded. 'Can you say categorically that the cut throat was the cause of death?'

Sullivan met the detective's hazel eyes with a touch of amusement. 'Ninety per cent of me says yes, Alex, but wait until I've done the post-mortem.' He made another attempt at levity. 'Just in case he had a heart attack halfway through.'

'Right to left or left to right?'

The pathologist winced. 'Again, I'm guessing,' he said. 'But it *looks* like right to left.' He fore-stalled the detective's next question. 'And judging by the spray on the ceiling, he was standing about here and was looking up to see who was coming.' He moved towards the base of the steps. 'The assault *looks* . . .' again he stressed the word, 'like it was done by a right-handed man, and it was committed from the front.' He met the detective's eyes. Neither man needed to point out the fact that the assailant's clothes must have been splashed with a considerable amount of blood.

'Any idea when the PM will be?' Randall asked the question almost casually. He had already exerted enough pressure on Dr Sullivan.

'I can fit him in first thing Monday morning, Alex. Have you let Martha know?'

Randall nodded and Mark Sullivan picked up on something – embarrassment? He scrutinized his colleague. DI Randall was well known for being a very private man. Little was known about his personal life. He didn't even know if the detective was married – or not. And Martha had been widowed more than fifteen years ago.

39

Sullivan narrowed his eyes. Were the detective's interests lying in that direction? Now that was interesting. But then Martha was a very attractive woman with a sparky character to match her flaming red hair. For himself, Dr Sullivan was feeling pretty jaunty. After some wretched years of marriage to the alcoholic who had dragged him into her pit of vipers, he had finally broken free. For almost a year he had been so relieved to be rid of her that he had simply revelled in his freedom.

And then . . . Sullivan smiled to himself. It was early days yet but he had a feeling. Oh, the internet was a wonderful thing. After kissing a few female frogs he had met someone who right from the very start had felt special. He fingered his mobile phone. On silent mode, he had felt it vibrate and was certain there was a message from her. Instant messaging meant instant happiness. Something which had eluded him until now.

He looked sharply at the DI, trying to read his mind. 'I'll ring Martha if you like,' he said kindly, 'and leave a message with Jericho about my initial findings.'

Randall nodded and Sullivan left to return to the hospital or the mortuary, his more familiar stomping grounds.

It was time for the initial briefing. Randall turned around and headed for the Incident Room.

He currently had only a small number of officers working with him. It was early days yet. More would arrive *if* or rather *when* needed. They could all hope for an early conclusion but he already had a feeling this case would turn out to be complicated.

He cleared his throat and the room stilled.

'OK,' he said. 'We have an unidentified male aged somewhere between forty and fifty. Medium height, medium build, brown hair streaked with grey. No ID. Apparently no personal belongings. Looks as if he's been sleeping rough for some time.' Randall recalled ragged nails, neglected stubble, the general air of the unwashed. A scent as powerful, repellent and unmistakable as that of putrefaction. 'Apparent cause of death a single slash across the throat. Obviously this'll be confirmed or refuted by a post-mortem which is provisionally scheduled for Monday morning.'

He wrote a list of priorities on the whiteboard. Time enough to ask for reinforcements, if the case turned out to warrant it. His personal instinct was that the most likely scenario was that this was a random killing, someone with a grudge against vagrants in general. The next possibility was that their unfortunate victim had stumbled across something more sinister, perhaps a drug deal. Failing that the third and, in his mind, least likely scenario was that this was a personal assault deliberately directed at their victim, in which case once they'd found out the man's identity the perpetrator would soon be found, possibly amongst the shifting population of the rootless. But the priority now was to await the results of the post-mortem, then to try and establish the man's identity so he could at least be named and his relatives contacted. Then he could be buried decently, with his name on a headstone. So, along

41

with gleaning every single shred of forensic evidence from the man's clothes, body and the crime scene, their first problem was to find out who he was.

Randall's second pressing problem was that access to the site wasn't great – a single track road with few passing places and some pretty treacherous pot holes. Bringing the forensic support van up here had been a nightmare, meeting farmers who were unwilling and unable to reverse their own unwieldy, huge trailers. Unless it was unavoidable it was better not to get too expansive with personnel in these initial stages. It would clog up the entire road system and annoy the few inhabitants of Moreton Corbet village.

He eyed the assembled officers. All tried and tested, male and female. Familiar faces. Trusted colleagues. Not a weak link amongst them, though there were a few dark horses and quite a few more family dramas lurking in the background, including his own. There'd be time to explore those issues in the future when events were less pressing. For now they needed to work together, as a team, without distraction.

'First of all,' he said, 'we need to liaise with English Heritage. The site will be closed to the general public until further notice. DC Shaw, perhaps you'll see to that?'

PC Delia Shaw nodded and made notes.

'Talith, you can work with Roddie Hughes supervising the crime scene and chain of custody of any forensic evidence.'

Like his colleague, Detective Sergeant Paul

Talith nodded without comment. He too knew exactly what was expected of him.

Randall continued, addressing PC Gary Coleman next. 'Coleman, start on the house-to-house, will you, speak to the neighbours, find out if this gentlemen was from around here or if they've seen him before.' He frowned. 'Or, for that matter, any other vagrants hanging around the place.

'PC Tinsley, get some artist's impressions of our man and get them to the press. Finding out this man's identity is of paramount importance. It may not lead us straight to his killer but it gives him the dignity of a name and maybe relatives who can supervise his funeral arrangements. See if you can get any witness statements.' He addressed the entire room. 'That goes for all of you. He must have got here somehow. His coat was dry but it's been raining intermittently for two days. We're eight miles from Shrewsbury, the nearest town. Perhaps our man hitch-hiked his way out here, in which case a couple of boards asking for information out on the main road might not go amiss. Or had he been here for more than two days?' He frowned, seeing the flaw in his argument already. He couldn't picture John Hyde failing to spot him on his almost daily visits.

PC Lara Tinsley smiled but she too said nothing.

'See if you can get Dane Banks to draw some artist's impressions and get those out on the internet, will you?'

'Yes, sir.' Dane Banks was a fairly new acquisition, adept at taking likenesses from the dead in order to make the public aware. His pictures told a thousand words, or so his website advertised.

'PC Dart . . .' Randall's eyes rested on him thoughtfully. Now this was the wild card in his pack. PC Dart had come from Yorkshire with a personal request for an urgent transfer. And DI Randall reflected that if he, the SIO, had a secret backstory, then so did this junior officer, who similarly kept himself to himself, did not mix with his fellow officers or fraternize with his colleagues, or give out any personal information. PC Sean Dart returned his look coolly, almost bouncing back a challenge.

You keep your secrets, sir, and I get to keep mine.

Randall cleared his throat and continued to address the waiting officers. 'Get on the missing persons' website and see if you can come up with something, please? It would be nice to give this fellow a name.'

Dart merely nodded. Made no notes, Randall saw. He felt he needed to add something – to justify this directive.

'He may only have died sometime yesterday evening but if he was a vagrant he may have been reported missing in the past. He must have come from somewhere.'

Dart interrupted. 'Do we have a time of death, sir?'

Randall grimaced. 'Do we ever? Sometime between five and eleven p.m. last night.'

Dart smirked but Randall was frowning. As usual, he was trying to piece together the little they knew about the case so far. The man's coat had been dry. But yesterday it had rained heavily and steadily. It had been a dull, dark, thoroughly unpleasant evening, one where curtains would have been closed early, shutting everything out.

Great night for a murder, he thought and moved on, addressing the unfortunate PC Gethin Roberts next, who was still deathly pale.

'Roberts.'

The PC responded sharply. 'Yes, sir?'

'Go to the haunts of the homeless. Speak to the nuns at the convent. They give the vagrants a meal and the chance of some soap and hot water to wash in – if they choose to use it. See if they knew him. And don't forget McDonald's. The girls there can be pretty helpful and sympathetic towards their night visitors. They too may remember him.

'And Coleman, perhaps you'll see to the boards on the A53 and talk to the natives, will you?'

'Yes, sir.'

'I think that's it?' Randall scanned the room in case there were any forthcoming ideas but they all looked back at him steadily and he nodded. It was early days yet. 'OK,' he said. 'Report back here at eight p.m. If any of you have anything urgent or significant to report ring me on my mobile. Otherwise, wait until then. Off you go. Get on with it. Don't waste any more time.' His final bidding was spoken like an infant school teacher dismissing his class, with a note of indulgent admonishment lightening his instruction.

He watched them go. Hopefully one of his leads would at least lead them to the man's identity. And from there to the killer should be an easy step. He stood, staring at his whiteboard, and mused. What bothered him was the injury. A cut throat was hardly the result of a tramps' squabble, and the crime scene did not support the theory of a drunkard stumbling on an intruder when he had thought he would be sleeping alone. Again, Randall wondered: could a courting couple have turned on him, thinking he was a peeping Tom? Randall shook his head. The assault spoke of extreme violence. For his money he would bet on a couple of drug dealers. This had the mark of their form of violent crime. But surveillance of the general area around Shrewsbury was quite good. And to his knowledge this sort of drug dealer would not be found here but in the big cities: Stoke, Manchester, Birmingham and Glasgow rather than here.

None of these scenarios quite fitted with a cut throat. Had their tramp not carried a knife with him – and Randall had yet to come across a vagrant who did – the assailant must have been armed, weapon at the ready as he descended the steps. He shook his head, frustrated already. A cut throat was an unusual method of murder. The act had more connections with the Taliban or organized crime who liked gruesome methods of execution to warn off anyone who might challenge their authority.

A cut throat, in the criminal world, commanded respect.

His thoughts began to track away as he exercised his powers of observation and recollection. The man had been thin but not emaciated. Someone had been feeding him. The nuns provided one hot meal a day, McDonald's maybe more, but it was a precarious existence.

The coat had been a typical garment bought from a charity shop. Probably given away by a generous benefactor. Charity shop personnel were equally as likely as the nuns and the staff at McDonald's to be free with their gifts. After all, who wore these herringbone tweed thick wool coats these days? Expensive when new, unwanted second hand. Get caught out in the rain in one of these and they became instantly as heavy as a lead tabard, the ones the radiographers used to protect themselves from radiation. These days people tended to rely on anoraks or specialized outdoor clothing designed to breathe. Light, warm, waterproof, breathable as a pair of lungs. Randall's mouth twisted. He could almost spit out the adverts.

Now the area was as busy as a building site PC Gary Coleman could wander across the road and knock on the farmhouse door opposite the spectacular ruin which reminded him of the house in the final chapters of *Jane Eyre*. *Thornfield Hall*. That was it. He could imagine a mad woman dancing on the ramparts as it had burned. But then this place hadn't had a fire, had it? It just hadn't ever quite been finished. And that, according to the stories, was all due to superstition. Coleman spluttered derisively. A curse. He was modernist, a computer lover. For him curses didn't exist, but even so he wouldn't like to confront this spooky old ruin every time he opened *his* front door.

47

As he waited for the farm door to be answered he looked up at the black-and-white walls of the farmhouse. Farmers were always protesting that they were poor. He gave a huff of disagreement. It didn't look like that to him. If this was poor, what the hell was he? Working his balls off to afford a small semi in the town, saving for the dream wedding he'd always wanted. Oh, yes. Patty would have it. A *big* diamond, the *perfect* wedding and then a year or two later, when he'd paid it all off, *a little one on the way*? He scratched his chin and banged on the door again.

It was pulled open by a tall, thin man with sharp eyes and a beaky nose. He was dressed in an old navy sweater and olive-green corduroy trousers. His feet were encased in cream woollen socks. He was wearing no shoes and his facial expression was politely inquisitive. 'Yes?'

Coleman displayed his ID and began in a round-about way, 'Mr . . .?'

'Sharp,' the man supplied crisply. 'Rufus Sharp.' To Coleman he sounded posh. He eased in gently to his narrative.

'You may have noticed some activity at the castle, sir?'

'I'd have to be bloody blind not to,' Sharp barked. 'What's going on? Police cars every-where, frightening the cattle.'

Irritated now rather than curious, Coleman noted. 'We've found a body in the cellar, sir.'

The man frowned. 'A body?'

'Yes, sir.'

'What – someone's had a heart attack?' He guffawed as though this was the funniest thing

48

he could have said. 'Overcome by the spectacular ruin that should have been pulled down years ago? Bloody dangerous place, if you ask me.'

Coleman gaped. Everyone so far had been making a big thing about what a fantastic, historic, beautiful and wonderful place Moreton Corbet Castle was. And here was this man saying it should be pulled down? He didn't get it.

'We don't think it was a heart attack,' he said cautiously. 'The pathologist thinks . . .' He was skipping around the truth, trying to conceal what was not yet in the public domain. 'He thinks the man probably didn't die from natural causes.' Inwardly Coleman was groaning at his ineptitude. It was always difficult at this early stage of the investigation to gauge just how much potential suspects should be told. Nothing if he had his way, he thought grumpily.

'So what exactly did he die of?' Sharp scrutinized him. 'You're not saying he was murdered, are you?'

These were just the questions Coleman didn't want to answer. *Keep the buggers in the dark* was his motto.

The gentleman farmer glowered at him. 'What exactly *are* you saying, Constable?'

Coleman declined to answer, doggedly pursuing his own line of questioning. 'Did you see anyone at the castle last night?'

Sharp thought about it only briefly. 'No,' he said flatly, adding, 'at least I don't think so. But it was a rainy night and my living rooms all face the back.' He gave a yellow-toothed grin. 'So I wouldn't have, would I?'

Although riled Coleman answered steadily, controlling his response. 'Just asking, sir,' he said woodenly.

'Who was the man?' Sharp at last showed delayed curiosity.

'We don't know his identity yet but . . .' Coleman was struggling. 'It's possible he was a vagrant.'

Sharp looked affronted. 'A tramp?'

'It's possible, sir. Have you seen anyone looking like a vagrant hanging around there?'

'No, I bloody haven't,' Sharp said. 'If I had I'd have taken my blunderbuss to him.'

Gary Coleman gaped and Sharp laughed. 'Only a joke, Constable. Just a joke.'

But looking at Sharp's face, he wasn't convinced.

Six

PC Delia Shaw, in the meantime, was initially having an easier time speaking on the telephone to Gilbert Warrilow from English Heritage. He was proving much more amenable than Sharp.

But then she, unlike Coleman, had had had some time to practise her lines because it had taken her a while to track him down.

She began by introducing herself before launching into an explanation. 'Unfortunately, sir, we've found a body in suspicious circumstances at Moreton Corbet Castle,' she said, hurrying on to her point, 'and so for the moment, I'm afraid we're going to have to keep the entire site closed to the public.'

There was a moment of stunned silence, then Warrilow asked, 'How long for?'

Delia Shaw, who was tact personified, answered, 'Regretfully, sir, until we have finished with the site.' She paused. 'I can't say how long that will be.' Maybe, she thought, she'd better prepare him. 'It can take a few weeks, sir.'

There was a moment of stunned silence before Warrilow gave a loud scraping of his throat. 'Well,' he harrumphed. 'What will be will be. I don't suppose there's any point my objecting, is there, Constable Shaw? It won't make any difference, will it? You're hardly going to stop the investigation of a . . .' he paused as though either

51

doubting or mocking her initial words, '. . . *suspicious death* just because the site of the villainy is also a site of historic significance, are you?' He gave a bark of uncertainty before saying crisply, 'I take it you'll be courteous enough to keep me informed of any developments?'

'Of course we will, sir.' Her voice now was soothing, reassuring, placating.

'And I also take it that there will be no damage done to the structure?' Another bark of embarrassment before he added, 'Poor old castle's had a bad enough time in the past.'

PC Delia Shaw was perfectly aware that she could *not* give a guarantee that there would be no damage done to the structure of the castle. What if they needed to scrape off some of the stone work to get stains analysed at the lab? In previous investigations she'd seen doors ripped off hinges, stones or bricks chipped out of walls or removed completely, sometimes to reappear as evidence in a courtroom, and paint scraped away from window frames. Window frames themselves removed to be brought into court as dumb witnesses to demonstrate opening and shutting. And what if they needed to dig below the foundations?

She took a deep breath in and did her best. 'We will do all we can to preserve the site, sir.'

'And what exactly does that mean?'

His tone had sharpened and Delia tried again to pour oil on troubled waters. 'Please, sir, don't worry.'

There was a brief, disapproving silence before Warrilow gave a bark of acquiescence. 'I don't suppose I've got any choice, have I?'

'Not really, sir.' Shaw tried to inject even more sympathy into her voice but really it was all used up on the murdered man. She'd caught a glimpse of the pathetic figure in the thick, grubby coat many sizes too big for his gaunt frame. She'd seen his terrible wound, his white face, the eyes which seemed to appeal to her from underneath drooped lids. Finally she had seen this poor man zipped into a body bag and driven away, knowing he would be unzipped in the mortuary when the pathologist was ready to perform the post-mortem. All these images had stayed with her. She only hoped they would not continue to haunt her.

She gave out more meaningless reassurance, promised to keep him informed and rang off.

PC Gary Coleman, meanwhile, having got little help out of Sharp – nothing but denial and innocence and no information at all – had crossed the road to the cream-coloured cottage next to the castle. He knocked for a while but wasn't hopeful of a response. The place looked deserted. There were no cars in the drive. Owners out at work, he supposed and slipped a card through the letter box requesting that they contact him as soon as possible.

Then he thought he'd better check out the church which was, unusually these days, unlocked. He unlatched the heavy oak door and stepped inside, breathing in the scent of musty old books, wax candles and altar cloths and, oddly, his grandmother who, until her death, had been an ardent churchgoer. Did they all sprinkle themselves with the same lavender water? he wondered.

Light streamed in through the stained-glass windows, throwing bright pools of light on to the floor to dance around his feet. He stepped inside, shut the door and made his way up the aisle, half closing his eyes, imagining. Now this was exactly the sort of church he wanted to get married in. He was so busy picturing Patty swanning up the aisle towards him, her face wreathed in delighted smiles that her day had come or else shrouded by a veil – he never could decide which he preferred, face or veil – that he failed to notice the woman sitting right at the back wearing dark clothing, her head bowed, praying. His mind was absorbed with the froth of a white dress, the scent of roses and lilies, and yes, the lavender water too, six giggling bridesmaids and his mates in suits ragging him and making silly speeches.

Still unseen, the woman slipped out.

PC Gary Coleman didn't even hear the latch. He was still mentally breathing in the church scents and hearing the sound of silk rustling, hymns playing, whispered comments.

When he came out of his reverie he was alone.

Police officers are not always as observant as they might be.

Focusing on the last four years, PC Sean Dart was sitting at a computer searching through files of missing persons. There was a depressing number of them. Children (just a few), teenagers (plenty of them) and women and men (mostly middle- aged but a few elderly). He concentrated his search on Shropshire, frowning into the screen, hunting for the man. It seemed odd to

54

him that they could only call him that generic name: The Man. They could not call him anything yet. Not Jack or Tim or Steven. Not even John Doe. He was, for the moment anyway, simply The Man, and it seemed important to dignify his death by finding out his name. Dart's dark eyes scanned the screen. He couldn't see him here. Not on this file.

The Man wasn't staring at him from the screen declaring himself. But then four years, Shropshire. It was a narrow parameter. The man could have joined the army of vagrants years ago. He could have come from anywhere. He might not even be British. Maybe he wasn't in any of these files. Maybe no one had cared enough to report him missing. Sean Dart leaned back in his chair to think and try to understand someone who wanted to detach themselves from their previous life. He, of all people, should be able to understand this decision. It was exactly what he had done. He widened his search criteria, extended his period of time, worked through file after file, studying this army of vanished people, looking at known details, whereabouts, sightings, possible reasons for their disappearance. There were plenty: alcohol, drugs, marital breakup, mental illness, redundancy, financial ruin, to escape justice, family feuds, to escape debt, to escape the law, to escape someone who wanted to kill them.

Dart pushed back his chair. Now that was an interesting one. To escape someone who wanted to kill you. He leaned forward again, anxious to look closer. There was a case right here of a man somewhere in his forties. Possible reason for disappearance? Two a.m. one night, drunk, he had hit a teenage girl who herself had been on a drunken night out in the town. She had staggered into the road, in front of the car and had subsequently lost both her legs plus, the synopsis said, her entire nose and the sight of one eye. PC Sean Dart sat still in his chair, thinking. The girl's father had vowed he would kill him and Daniel Kamara, the driver in question, had subsequently vanished. No court case. No conviction. No prison sentence. Kamara had joined the ranks of the disappeared. Suspecting foul play or even suicide, the local police force in Market Drayton had made a substantial search of the surrounding area and of the home of the girl, called Noona Parry. They had found nothing. They had spent hours questioning her father. (Her mother was, apparently absent. Not missing, the investigating team had been assured. She was in Cyprus with an ex-solider.)

Sean Dart brought up a picture of Daniel Kamara who would, by now, have been forty-eight years old. But there was no way he could be the man who had died in Moreton Corbet Castle. For a start, he was bald, whereas The Man had had a full head of hair. More than that – a full head of very long, greasy hair. Shame, Dart thought, it would have been great to have been the one to find out his identity. But, he realized, it was possible that the story of The Man taking to the streets would be just such a sorry tale, a story with a backstory and behind that another tragic story. Kamara's wife had subsequently taken up with a wealthy local businessman and . . . Dart's smile broadened. Here was an interesting twist of fate. When he Googled the man's name – more for idle curiosity than anything else – amongst other things, such as where he'd gone to school and so on, his involvement with various charities was listed. And hey ho. Here was one of them. *Missing: the local charity for the homeless*. And the man? Graham Knebworth. Not known to the police.

He studied Kamara's picture again, willing it to somehow be The Man. But no. It definitely wasn't him. It couldn't be him.

Pity. It would have been so neat. And he, for once, would be the hero instead of PC Sean 'Dark Horse' Dart. He knew what they called him here just because he kept his past a secret. But if he cracked this one, instead of looking at him askance, his fellow officers, male and female would be slapping his back in congratulation, offering to buy him beers. But no. He turned away from the image. It wasn't to be.

He returned to the more general search and came up with a depressing number of teenagers who were either in care or had quarrelled with their mother, their father, their mother's or father's new partner and had simply upped sticks and left. Teenage pique.

And so these people vaporized, whatever their reasons, leaving behind families who were confused, questioning everything they thought they'd ever known about their mum, their dad, their son or daughter. And sometimes they just didn't care. Some of the comments recorded were not just negative. They were damning.

He was a waste of space . . . Trouble from the start . . . He's not missed . . . Best thing he ever did, going AWOL . . . And finally, the most cruel of epitaphs. *Hope he stays away.*

Dart stood up, agitated. There had been a time when he would have liked to have disappeared too. Then what would they have said about him, the people who had known him? Which one of these withering comments would have been hurled after his disappearing form?

PC Gethin Roberts had driven smartly into Shrewsbury, parked up in Abbey Foregate and was currently talking to the nuns at the Holy Cross Catholic Church. They provided the homeless with a hot meal every single day, Christmas and Easter with no exception, privacy and hot water to wash and, if wanted, a kindly ear to listen. Roberts had imagined them in a thoroughly stereotypical way – quoting the Bible at their clients, pontificating or even trying to convert them. But they were none of these. It was true the door was opened by a nun in a traditional habit and she spoke quietly. Initially the Mother Superior's blue eyes sparkled with interest at his precised account of trying to find the identity of a man who had died, but when he explained in more detail what his mission was her blue eyes became unbearably sad, as though she saw the sins of the world behind the act. She gave a long sigh and her shoulders drooped.

'Evil,' she said. 'To take a life is pure evil. The men and few women who come here are peaceable. They wish no harm to anyone. For reasons

58

of their own they simply want to live their lives in anonymity. It distresses me that one of our flock has met with such a violent end.' She lifted her eyes to him. 'I shall pray for him.'

'We don't know that this man was one of your flock,' Roberts said. He felt very slightly uncomfortable with the nun, who was aged somewhere in her sixties but with an unlined face. Not the result of a facelift, he guessed shrewdly.

'They are all our flock,' she said. Then repeated, 'Are all our flock.'

Roberts then produced the artist's picture which had been produced and hurried through from their photographs taken at the scene. The Mother Superior gazed at it then looked up, her face puzzled. 'I'm not sure,' she said. 'I shall show it to my sisters.' She disappeared out of the room, returning minutes later, a small, younger nun following, her eyes downcast. The Mother Superior spoke for her. 'Sister Agnes believes she might know something of this man,' she said and prompted her. 'Speak, Sister Agnes.'

The nun was older than the Mother Superior. Much older. To Roberts she looked about a hundred. Underneath her wimple her face was aged and lined but tranquil. She had a face you could trust. She handed the picture back to PC Gethin Roberts, who felt his pulse start to race. She knew something. He could see it in her shrewd blue eyes. Was *he* to be the one who discovered the man's identity?

Normally he would already be planning on telling Flora, his long-term girlfriend, of his success, embellishing his story richly as he went.

But today he felt a skip of apprehension. While *his* plans had raced towards a wedding, a mortgage and children, Flora, it seemed, had been battling with her own demons. He'd always noticed that when he started talking about this future she'd go quiet. Sometimes she'd say that she wasn't sure about it, or that she didn't want to get married. Not yet and why didn't they stay like they were?

Then, finally, last Saturday, she'd sat him down and told him . . . and he'd had to rethink his entire future. It might not be like that, she'd said. And he was having a real problem adjusting. In fact, he didn't know what to do. He forced himself to focus on the nun's words.

'He wasn't one of our regulars,' she was saying.

Sister Agnes, he thought, had the sweetest voice he'd ever heard. It rang, sincere and clear, true as a bell. Each word was uttered slowly.

She continued. 'And he kept himself to himself.'

'Do you know his name?'

She shook her head.

'Do you know where he came from?'

Another negative shake of the head.

'Did he have a regional accent?'

At least she thought about this before she shook her head again.

'Mention any family?'

'No.'

'Did he come in on a regular day?'

'No. Sometimes not for months and then two days in a row.'

'Did he have any friends, someone he would chat to?'

Somehow Roberts had already guessed the answer to this: another shake of the head.

'Do you know how long he's been coming here?'

'Not really.'

'A year?'

'More than that, I think.'

'Five years?'

'Possibly. We have some who have been homeless for many years.'

Roberts reflected. It was a long time to be in such a position. He tried to steer the interview away from the general back towards the specific. He wanted to be sure he had extracted all information from these two nuns. They had known The Man – alive – if they were right about who he was. He needed to be sure.

'This man is aged forty to fifty. He is thin . . .'

Mother Superior smiled. 'They all are,' she said softly. 'Sleeping rough, managing on the one meal that we give them. They don't get fat on that.'

Roberts swallowed and ploughed on. 'Does this still sound like our man?' He indicated the picture.

She nodded.

Roberts moved on. 'He was wearing a thick tweed herringbone coat that was too big for him.'

Sister Agnes nodded.

'And suit trousers.'

Something flickered in her eyes. Recognition.

'Suit trousers,' Roberts repeated, watching her carefully for her response before continuing. 'And black leather shoes, one with a red lace.'

The Mother Superior sank into her chair, looking grave. 'And he was murdered. How?'

Roberts started to protest, 'Now, you know I can't . . .'

But she stopped him with her hand.

'And you tell me you don't know his name?'

'He had no name,' Sister Agnes said.

'But everyone . . .'

'Most people do have some sort of name,' she agreed. 'Frequently not their real name. They choose to call themselves Robert or Peter or Tim or Charles – or whatever. But this man had no name. He called himself nothing. He would not answer to any epithet and he refused to engage with any of us; there was never an explanation.'

'Was he a . . .'

She met his eyes and anticipated his question. 'No, Constable,' she said firmly. 'He was not a drunk. He was intelligent. He had a nice voice.'

'A regional accent?' Roberts asked again in frustration.

She shook her head. 'He could have been from anywhere,' she said. 'He was classless. Accentless.'

Fucking anonymous, Roberts thought. And almost smiled at the thought of the response had he added this to the list out loud.

'Do you know the circumstances behind his homelessness?'

'No. He never spoke of them. Most don't, you know.'

'When did you last see him?'

'I'll have to ask the others,' Sister Agnes said

62

gently. 'I don't spend as much time talking with them as I'd like.'

Roberts stood his ground. 'If you would,' he said politely.

But the Mother Superior dismissed him with a firm, 'We'll be in touch if we have any more information for you.'

'Thank you. One last question . . .' He didn't even know why he was asking this. It was surely not even slightly relevant? 'Was he a Catholic?'

'Yes, he was.'

Now he knew something about him. 'So he went to confession?'

But the Mother Superior was too clever for him. She could see exactly where this was heading. 'You know the rules of the confessional,' she said.

'Which surely can be broken if the man had been murdered and it might help to find his killer?'

'Confession made to a priest is between the man and his God,' she said primly.

Roberts knew when he was beaten. He cast around in his mind for another question and came up with . . . precisely nothing. 'Thank you,' he said and bowed his head.

The Mother Superior saw him out. 'Unfortunately people – some people,' she corrected, 'see these poor unfortunates as a legitimate target for aggression. We have had a few others attacked and one last year died of his injuries.'

'I don't remember that,' Roberts said.

The Mother Superior gave a grim smile. 'Well,

it wasn't exactly a hard case to solve. Joseph Gallagher was – to be honest – quite a drinker. He came out of a pub one night the worse for wear. It was all captured on the town cameras. He was talking . . .'

Roberts translated. *Shooting his mouth off.*

'Talking,' she repeated as though she'd heard his silent thought. 'Making political comments, I believe. Some other drinkers took exception to this and basically beat him up. He died in hospital of his injuries.'

Roberts knew he'd have to look into it.

Seven

PC Lara Tinsley had drafted out an email to their local and national press associates. She was reading it through.

> *Early this morning the body of a Caucasian man aged between forty and fifty was found in suspicious circumstances at Moreton Corbet Castle in Shropshire. The police are currently working on the assumption that he died sometime on Thursday evening. At the moment the police believe that the man was either a vagrant or homeless and his death is thought to be the result of foul play. A post-mortem has been arranged for Monday morning when more details will be released. Would anyone who believes they have information please call this number. All information will be treated confidentially.*

Beneath she put her contact details.

She looked at it, and felt something was lacking. Yeah – like who is this man? She made a face and pressed send. Almost immediately she watched as messages started pinging back in and her phone started ringing. The press had instant access to anything coming from the police. Crime was news. News sold papers. She made a face and started batting away questions on the internet and from the other end of her phone, placed in front of her on speaker phone. She could tell them little more.

She had one ironic thought: this would surely raise the profile of the little-known ruin! It would draw crowds to gape at that dramatic and beautiful facade. The ruin would now have a contemporary tragedy. Families would picnic out on the Murder at Moreton Corbet Castle. It would assume an even greater place in Shropshire folklore.

Roberts was deciding whether to treat himself to chicken nuggets and French fries or whether it would appear unprofessional to be munching away at the same time as he was questioning the staff at McDonald's.

He initially asked the girls who were busy dishing out the orders and was soon speaking to the supervisor, a neat, polite lad in his late twenties with the name 'Jim' printed on his name badge. He eyed Roberts suspiciously and came up with the unoriginal line, spoken pleasantly, 'And how may I help you?'

Roberts gave him a potted version of events and told 'Jim' that they were trying to find out the identity of a homeless man found dead in Moreton Corbet Castle.

Jim raised his eyebrows and said precisely nothing.

Roberts realized he was probably worried that he and his staff would get into trouble for sheltering and feeding vagrants in the establishment.

Roberts tried to reassure him. 'Look,' he said reasonably, 'we just want to find out who he was.'

'Well, my girls are good to the homeless,' Jim said. 'I mean – what's the harm?'

'I couldn't agree more,' Roberts said, wishing the food didn't smell so tempting. 'I think it's wonderful that you're so kind to them.' He tried a feeble joke. 'I bet Ronald McDonald would approve, really.'

Jim didn't even attempt to raise a smile.

Roberts showed him the picture and Jim took a good hard look. 'Can't say I know him. Look,' he said. 'Can I have a copy? I'll show it round the girls and see if I can come up with something.'

Roberts almost hugged him. 'Sure,' he said. 'Got a photocopier?'

Friday, 12 September, 8 p.m.

There wasn't really much to report at this stage, although each officer related the results of their afternoon's work. But they all knew they were waiting for the post-mortem. Waiting for forensic evidence to be gathered and analysed, waiting for someone to come forward with knowledge of The Man's identity.

Roberts went through the response at the convent, mentioning that Sister Agnes appeared to have known him but hadn't given much else in the way of information. He told them about another homeless man who'd been attacked and

67

died from his injuries – Joseph Gallagher. A few officers used their iPads and smartphones to search through the details. Gallagher had died following a drunken brawl outside a pub. Most of the fracas had been captured on CCTV. Gallagher had been staggering, lashing out, and four men had responded. Gallagher's body had sustained twenty-eight separate injuries. All four men had been arrested, two of the ringleaders charged with manslaughter and sentenced and the other two had somehow been gifted non-custodial sentences.

The ways of the law.

The general feeling was that the crimes were different, the only common factor being that both victims had been homeless.

With satisfaction, Roberts watched DI Randall write up the little they knew about The Man on the whiteboard. They wrote *The Man* at the top.

Underneath that: *Catholic? Five years a vagrant? Kept himself to himself. Didn't give away his name.*

'Why not?' Randall threw the question out into the room and got some response.

'Someone famous?'

'Somebody after him?' That from PC Dart, who quickly related the story of Daniel Kamara.

More suggestions were tossed into the room to be considered.

'He's known to the law?'

They weren't short of ideas.

Coleman went through Sharp's reaction to the murder and PC Tinsley read out her press release. Although they were almost certain of the cause of death they hoped that the post-mortem would somehow help their investigation.

Alex Randall wound up the briefing and the officers dispersed. But not all of them had finished their day's work.

Friday, 12 September, 9 p.m.

Gary Coleman received the call in the evening. Wilfred Hook, the owner of Moreton Corbet Cottage, and Imogen had arrived home.

Wilfred Hook sounded energetic, bouncy and full of enthusiasm, even at the news of the murder. 'Poor chap,' he said, and Coleman heard him shout, presumably to his wife. 'Feller died at the castle, Imogen.'

There was no rejoinder and Mr Hook continued asking more questions to which virtually all Coleman's answers were *don't know* or *can't tell*. And thinking, *I wouldn't tell you even if I did know the answer.*

'Who was the man? How did he die? Is foul play suspected?'

And so on.

Finally Coleman arranged to interview them in the morning, when he would bring a picture – or photofit – of The Man.

Wilfred Hook rang off with a sobering comment. 'S'pose I'd better be careful I lock up properly tonight. Eh, Imogen?'

Again, there was no rejoinder.

Eight

Friday, 12 September, midnight.

It had fallen to Sergeant Sandy Mucklow to guard the crime scene together with a young special constable called Dean Kramer. Kramer was angling after a permanent place in the force so was always volunteering for something or other. The truth was that his application had been treated favourably largely on the strength of his prowess on the rugby field. He was a big guy with the heart of a chicken and he was finding, even with his sergeant's comfortable and sturdy presence, this place too spooky by half. It didn't help that the moon was strolling across a sky blotted with huge clouds so one minute it appeared, lighting the scene with silver, and the next minute they were in total darkness. And it didn't help either that a tawny owl was 'whoo-whoo'-ing from a nearby tree. To cover up his unease, Kramer started telling Mucklow about various tries he'd performed playing for his team, which were hardly from the top division – Newport, Shropshire – not even Newport Gwent. Truth was Mucklow was bored stiff as Kramer rambled on. 'I just picked up the ball. And I ran and ran. I could hear everyone screaming and shouting.' Kramer's eyes gleamed in sudden moonlight. 'I had the wind at my back and it was lifting me. Right to the touchline. I was deafened by the roar. Never forgotten it.'

Mucklow made a non-committal grunt. He was tired. He would have given anything for a nice warm bed and someone to cuddle up to. But that particular wish was not to be granted. His long-term girlfriend had left two years ago, her words still echoing sharp as glass in his ears. *'You're never there, Sandy. Your wife is the force. Get it? I'm superfluous so stay married to your "wife". I'm off to find myself a man who spends at least some time with me. Appreciates me. Understand?'*

What was there to understand? he thought gloomily. In some ways she was right. Look where he was now.

Kramer was still rambling on. 'If I hadn't slipped just at that exact moment I'd have been playing for England by now. I would. I'd have been in the team.'

'Yeah,' said Mucklow, still unenthusiastic.

They'd made themselves a sort of base in the Great Tower. Moonlight, Gothic ruin. The scene was set. Strange to think it had been around for nine hundred years. Kramer stopped talking and screwed up his face. Nine hundred years. He looked around, thoroughly spooked now. What had Shropshire been like nine hundred years ago? He tried to imagine a world without cars, without mobile phones, without television – and failed completely.

Imagination was not Kramer's strongest point. But it did strike him as incredible that after nine hundred years here they were, in this dramatic-looking ruin, and even with all modern technology at their disposal: DNA, fingerprints, computer databases that contained just about every personal detail of almost everyone in the United Kingdom and most of the rest of the world as well, they had not managed to identify their man. The damn owl 'whoo-whoo'ed again and Kramer was startled back into the present. 'What was that?' His voice sounded strained after the monotonic match commentary. He fingered his mobile phone. Lifeline? Not really. If the killer was still around and wanted blood, however quick the response to a 999 call they would be too late. He fingered his own thick neck uncomfortably then looked at Mucklow. Mucklow, too, had heard or seen something. He had stiffened, tensed up, head forward listening intently.

Something was moving amongst the buildings. Clutching speedcuffs, pepper spray, batons, personal radios and flashing their torches, they aimed the beams. The words of the news bulletin echoed around uncomfortably. *This man is dangerous. If you see him do not approach but summon help.*

Trouble was he and Mucklow here *were* the help.

The moon had helpfully emerged from behind the cloud at just the right time, casting a shadow of the facade on to the mown grass. They picked out the moving shape – a badger – and missed the other shape – a woman, standing at the gate. Just standing. She'd been drawn back to the scene, as though it was magnetic, had parked her car two hundred yards away and now softly walked back.

Nine

Saturday, 13 September, 9.30 a.m.

Gary Coleman watched the estate car swing into the drive. The occupant of Moreton Corbet Cottage had arrived home. He walked up towards the house and encountered Wilfred Hook inserting the key in his door to the accompaniment of some loud, welcoming barks.

Hook turned to look at him. 'Hello? Just been out to get the paper.'

Coleman introduced himself, displaying his ID card, and Hook met his eyes. He was a plump man, soft bellied and bald, with a beneficent face. He reminded Coleman of a sofa stuffed with duck-down. Even his voice was soft. 'Obviously I've seen all the comings and goings. I'm intrigued. Are you going to explain?'

'Certainly, sir,' Coleman said smartly. 'Shall we go inside?'

Imogen turned out to be a beautiful Golden Labrador who welcomed her master with affection and enthusiasm before turning her attention on the police officer.

When he and Patty were married, he thought, after the wedding, once they had a house and just before they started a family, he would very much like a dog just like this one. He bent and patted the hound, who wagged her tail in appreciation.

Hook led him into a small, chintzy sitting room which smelt of dog and Coleman began his explanation. 'As I told you, the body of a man has been found in the castle,' he said.

Hook showed only mild curiosity. 'Whereabouts?'

'In the cellar off the lower chamber of the dining hall.'

'So . . .?' Hook didn't appear shocked or even surprised. Coleman had to remind himself that Mr Wilfred Hook didn't know the full story – yet. He'd skipped round any facts last night, deflecting his questions with *don't know*s or *can't tell*s. Now he could fill in some of the detail.

'We're still waiting for the official results of the post-mortem,' he said guardedly, 'but his injuries are consistent with homicide. He'd had his throat cut, sir.'

Hook made a shocked face and bent to stroke the dog. 'And he was killed here?'

'We're working on that theory.'

Hook was silent for a long minute, his face twisting and his mouth stern. Something of her master's concern appeared to translate to the dog. She sat still, her head now on her master's lap, tail not wagging any more. Her mournful brown eyes looked up into his face.

Hook patted her absent-mindedly, then looked straight at PC Coleman. 'This is awful,' he said. 'Who could have done such a horrible thing?' Then he frowned. 'Who was the man?'

'We don't know,' Coleman said frankly. 'We're

75

currently working on the assumption that he was a vagrant, a tramp.'

Hook gave a long, deep sigh. 'Poor man,' he said. Then added, 'Horrible. Quite horrible.' His hand moved towards his own neck, 'Am I in any danger, Constable?'

'Two police will be guarding the site for the next couple of days,' Coleman said, 'but in my experience most killers want to put as much distance between them and their crime as possible. I would, however, suggest that you're careful to keep doors and windows locked and contact us if you see anything suspicious.' Coleman frowned. 'Do you live alone?'

The question appeared to cause Hook some discomfort. 'Except for Imogen.' He gave Coleman a bold, defiant stare.

Gary Coleman had looked at the electoral register and seen that two years ago there had been a Mrs Hook. A Mrs Mavis Hook. So where had she vanished to?

It would do for another time, but the fact was that Wilfred, however urbane and pleasant he might appear, had been right here, on the scene, as near as it was possible to be.

'Just for the record,' he asked casually, 'where were you on Thursday night?'

'The marquetry club. In Shrewsbury,' Hook answered quickly and brightly. 'Second Thursday every month – except Christmas and New Year, of course.'

'And you get back at what time?'

'About ten thirty. We usually stop and have a bit of a drink, you know.'

'You mean the other members of the marquetry club?'

'Yes. There are ten of us.'

'I see.' So Hook had an alibi.

Coleman smiled. 'Just checking, you understand.' Something struck him. 'When you drove home—'

Hook interrupted. 'It was a nasty night. Pouring it down. I was glad to get back, actually.'

'You didn't notice anyone at the side of the road?'

Hook frowned, scowling to remember. 'Don't think so,' he said.

Coleman bent and patted Imogen. 'And did you take Imogen out for a walk when you got back?'

'Always do,' Hook said, then stopped himself. 'Ah.'

PC Gary Coleman pursued his prey. 'Did you notice anything out there?'

Hook shook his head. 'No, I didn't,' he said.

'Have you ever seen someone scruffy, a tramp maybe, hanging around here?'

'Once or twice. Never took much notice. What was it our Lord said – the poor are always with us?'

Coleman nodded then showed him the artist's impression of The Man. 'Have you ever seen him around here before?'

Hook shook his head. 'Not that I remember. Of course, you don't look too carefully at vagrants.' He gave an embarrassed clearing of his throat. 'They always want . . .' His voice trailed off.

'Money,' Coleman supplied.

'Yes.' He paused. 'And they all look the same. Thick coats, long hair.' He looked up at Coleman. 'Same smell too.'

Coleman nodded.

'I do give them money sometimes,' Hook said. 'I know we're not supposed to because they spend any money on drugs or beer or whatever but he looked so wretched.'

Coleman pushed the picture closer to him.

'I don't think it was this man,' Wilfred Hook said. 'But you do feel sorry for them, don't you?'

Coleman nodded. He was aware that Wilfred Hook's attention was drifting away.

'We may ask you to take a look at the man's coat and see if you recognize it.'

Hook simply nodded.

'Sir,' he began again, and was aware that his information had triggered some response in Hook. 'Has anything like this ever happened before?'

Hook shook his head, but he was still preoccupied with something.

Coleman was in pursuit. 'Have you ever noticed anything suspicious happening around here?'

Again he shook his head but his expression was wary. 'Nothing much. You know, teenagers smoking, kids climbing the walls higher than they should. That sort of thing. Polystyrene food boxes and chucked away cans and papers.' He looked pained. 'It's that sort of place, Constable.' His eyes drifted back to the picture. 'But not this sort of place.'

Coleman knew he would get nothing more out of him.

Ten

The body of the man was wheeled into the post-mortem room still fully clothed. Everything on his body was to be recorded, photographed, bagged and kept as potential evidence. Now the bags were taken off his hands, swabs taken from underneath his fingernails and his fingerprints taken. Then the thick coat was removed and the pockets checked again. There wasn't much in there. A crumpled five-pound note, an apple core. The coat would be looked at carefully for any trace evidence of the assailant or perhaps a clue as to its origins. DI Randall watched the proceedings without comment until Talith felt along the lining.

'Something in here, sir,' he said. Randall bent over some neat hand stitching and felt a small object.

Talith cut through the stitching and pulled out a child's shoe. An old black leather object with a wooden sole nailed to the upper. A clog. It looked about a hundred years old and about the size a six-year-old would wear. The two police officers looked at each other, baffled. Mark Sullivan shrugged too. 'Search me,' he said. Then added thoughtfully, 'Do you think it's *his* child's shoe?'

79

Randall shook his head. 'It looks far too old. It looks Victorian or even older.' He studied it. 'I've seen something like it in museums. It can't be his own child's. At a guess it's over a hundred years old and handmade.'

The three men looked at each other, bemused.

'It looks too old to be his own father's, even.' Randall frowned. 'So I wonder whose it is and why he stitched it so carefully into his coat lining.'

'An heirloom?' Sullivan suggested.

Randall shook his head. 'Hardly,' he said. 'It's more of a peasant's shoe.'

'A reminder of something then?'

'Search me.'

Talith cleared his throat, embarrassed. 'Didn't I read somewhere that it was an ancient custom to bury a shoe in a house to keep the witches away?'

Not one of them laughed at this superstition. The image of the ruined house still clung to the body of this man. Somehow the idea of witches connected with the property didn't seem so ridiculous, even here, in the stark light of the mortuary. They all stared at the dead man's face and wondered.

Sullivan broke the silence, speaking to his assistant. 'Come on, Marcus. We've work to do.'

They removed the man's shoes next to expose a pair of holey socks through which both big toes poked. Big, fat toes with long, dirty nails curling beneath them. The feet stuck up looking almost ludicrous. Cartoon, holey socks. Feet, toes. There is no dignity in death.

Next they sliced off the man's grubby sweater,

carefully preserving the thick stain of blood around the neckline and found underneath it a cotton shirt with its collar undone. Compared to the coat and the sweater it was relatively clean apart from some blood around the collar. Underneath that was a grubby and smelly vest. His trousers were, like the coat, dirty with a dank, unwashed smell clinging to them and the pungent scent of stale urine.

'For once, Alex,' Mark Sullivan commented, looking up, 'I wouldn't mind you bringing me a nice, clean, hygienic corpse.'

'I'll do my best in future,' Randall muttered, but his eyes were fixed on the trousers. Like the coat, they must once have been expensive. They were good quality, pure 100% wool, the material heavy, partly hand stitched with a silk lining to the waistband. The maker's name was a Saville Row address. Randall might have been optimistic at this but he knew that, like the coat, they had probably been procured from a charity shop and held no clue at all to the man's identity. Still, he might hit lucky. Their man's underpants were similarly good quality but unpleasant to touch – slightly sticky even through gloves. Perhaps they had once been white, but it must have been a long, *long* time ago. Possibly when this guy last sat in a bath, he reflected.

Now naked, it was easier to see that their victim was underweight and bony, and there was a long surgical scar at the top of his right leg. 'This,' Sullivan said, fingering it, divining its message, 'could be of interest. It looks like he's had a pin and plate from a fractured shaft of femur, at a

81

guess.' He looked up, meeting their eyes to explain. 'Internal fixation. Usually the result of violent trauma in younger, fitter patients, and often associated with other injuries. We'll have full body X-rays. But, Alex, make no mistake about it: this is good news.'

Randall lifted his eyebrows and Mark Sullivan explained, 'Prostheses have ID numbers on them. We may be able to track him through this.'

Randall grinned at him then. 'Now that,' he said, 'could be very good news indeed for my budget. Could save a lot of time, Mark.'

Sullivan looked smug. 'Glad I can be of assistance, Alex. I think we'd better get on with the X-rays for now and see whether he's had any other trauma.'

Twenty minutes later Mark Sullivan was making a visual examination of the body, recording comments as he scrutinized the man. The comments would act as an *aide memoir* later when he was writing up the procedure. 'No tentative wounds,' he said, studying the man's forearms then looking across at the two detectives. 'Usually people have a couple of goes if they're about to slit their own throat.'

Talith winced.

'You said no weapon was found?'

Randall shook his head. 'No.'

'And we don't know whether he was right- or left-handed?'

Again Randall shook his head.

'So we can be certain this is a homicide.' Mark Sullivan looked up. 'Agreed?'

Both officers nodded.

'So,' Sullivan said, 'let's get to work.'

DI Alex Randall watched the pathologist as he had many times before. Deft fingers, no clumsiness any more. He wished the guy well. One day, four years ago, he had seen Dr Mark Sullivan slice through his finger with a scalpel when his hands had not been quite so steady.

Well, at least, Alex, he consoled himself, *you haven't resorted to drink. Yet.*

He had shed his revulsion at post-mortems years ago and now was simply an observer, making his own mental notes as the pathologist worked methodically.

Mark Sullivan began with the usual measurements and observations, taking blood samples before focusing on the man's main injury. Then he touched the gaping throat wound with the tip of his gloved index finger. 'Done with a bloody sharp knife,' he said. 'Probably a kitchen knife.' He risked a weak joke. 'Kitchen devil?' Then, as neither detective managed more than a half smile, he became more serious as he measured and probed. 'With an eight-inch blade. Not serrated. Say a meat knife?'

Randall nodded. 'Found in most kitchens.'

'This is a homicidal assault,' the pathologist said. 'Our man's head was directed upwards and the knife drawn across the throat in a quick, hard slash. Right to left. From the front, by a right-handed man.'

'You can be sure of that?'

'Yep. The cut is deeper on the right side and it's transverse rather than a "V". Deep all the way through, shallower on the left edge and done

83

with some force. There is a mark on the ante-vertebral muscle. One huge slash. There was nothing tentative about this. Nasty. Death would have been more or less instantaneous. Recalling the crime scene, I'd say he was practically dead when he staggered back, falling into the corner. The stains at his feet were residual oozing.'

He continued working, examining the brain, splitting the sternum to look at the heart and lungs, then moved to the man's leg which seemed to interest him most. 'Ha,' he said, pleased with himself. 'As I thought: old fractured shaft of femur. Spiral.' His voice slowed thoughtfully. 'Possibly as the result of a road traffic accident – maybe on a motor bike.' He probed further. 'Though it is a typical sportsman's injury.' He seemed to fish around, delicately slicing the skin as though filleting a fish, until some metal was exposed.

He studied it under a magnifying glass. 'Hm,' he said. 'Now that is interesting.'

Randall and Talith looked up, alerted.

'They haven't used this type of internal fixation for a long time. And never in the UK. I suspect your man had a skiing accident sometime in the late eighties, early nineties, somewhere abroad. It would fit in with both the injury and the use of this particular prosthesis.' He looked across at them. 'Young people are anxious to get up and about however bad the injury. They're not going to wait six weeks or more for a fracture to heal and then bang around on crutches and hang around while they work to get their fitness back. They want to be back on their skis.'

'So why don't we use these prostheses over here?' Talith asked, more out of curiosity than real interest.

It earned him Mark Sullivan's respect. 'The screws caused some damage on insertion and they were associated with problems later – pain and some readjustment of the leg length.'

Randall glanced at Talith, puzzled. The pathologist continued, 'What I'm saying is that your man here . . .' He touched the thigh, 'may have had a limp. There's some wasting of the muscles here; the right thigh is a tiny bit thinner than the left. And so on.'

'Can you say which countries did use this prosthesis?'

'Not without some research.' Sullivan was still looking jaunty. There was nothing he loved more than contributing his particular part to the investigation. 'But if I'm right and this was a skiing accident . . . Ah, yes.' He crossed to the computer screen and peered at the man's X-rays. 'Here,' he said, pointing and magnifying the image at the same time. 'Old wrist fracture. Scaphoid. Nasty one that, and associated with a fall on an outstretched hand. We'd have to look at Spain, France, Switzerland and the USA – basically anywhere where they do skiing.'

Randall was thoughtful. 'Are you saying,' he said slowly, 'that this guy is foreign?'

'Not necessarily. He could have been holidaying.' Mark Sullivan stood back and appraised him. 'He doesn't look foreign,' he said dubiously. 'I would have put him as IC1. White Caucasian.'

Randall was still thoughtful. He was trying to

form a profile of the man who lay on the slab, who had been brutally murdered. Homeless, a vagrant. Yet someone who'd been able to afford skiing holidays twenty or more years ago. He was building up a picture of a life – and a death.

'Any idea of his age, more precisely?'

'I'd say about forty-five.' Mark Sullivan peeled off his gloves. 'I can't be more certain than that.'

'Any other signs of illness or injury?'

Mark Sullivan grinned. He and Alex Randall had worked together so many times they knew each other's drill. He shook his head in answer. 'No,' he said. 'No distinguishing marks, no tattoos. No other traumas. Oh, and good teeth.'

'OK,' Randall said. 'Talith, you can go back to the incident room and see if anything's come up.'

'Yes, sir.'

'I think I'll head back via the coroner's office,' he said, discomfort making his voice awkward and heavy. 'Keep Martha filled in on the results of the post-mortem.'

'Good idea,' Sullivan said, struggling to keep the concern out of his voice.

He was pensive as he peeled off his gloves. Martha had no attachments as far as he knew. She'd never mentioned a boyfriend or partner. But Randall . . .? Mark Sullivan watched him go. His suspicions were growing, though he kept them to himself.

Eleven

Monday, 15 September, midday.

Martha was having a day when nothing seemed to be going well. People she needed to speak to were unavailable, doctors on annual leave, relatives similarly otherwise engaged. At the back of her mind was the issue of the man murdered in Moreton Corbet, apparently homeless – a vagrant. He was still anonymous. She wondered who he was and why someone had wanted to kill him. Had it been personal or a random killing? Was he truly one of the tramps one sometimes saw around the town or was he simply a scruffy local? Had they all jumped to the wrong conclusion? Her mind tussled with the endless possibilities. So she was fidgety and restless, and glad of Jericho's knock and his announcement that Detective Inspector Randall was wondering if he could have a word with her.

Gladly, she wanted to say but settled for a simple, 'Yes.' Not even tacking on, *of course*.

'Alex,' she said, rising when he entered the room. 'I'm so glad to see you. I've been thinking about that poor man.'

He waited until she had sat down again then settled comfortably into the armchair. 'I've just come from his post-mortem.'

'Oh. Any surprises?'

'Yes and no,' he said. 'He obviously died from a cut throat so no surprises there.'

'No,' she agreed.

'Cause of death, shock and haemorrhage due to the throat injury,' he said. 'No doubt about that either.'

'Any defensive wounds?'

'No.'

'Tentative wounds?'

Randall smothered a grin. He should have been well used to Martha's curiosity which, combined with her medical background, meant that she frequently showed a more than competent interest in her cases.

'Nothing except he'd had a broken leg in the past. Dr Sullivan thought it looked like an old skiing injury. It had had internal fixation.'

Martha frowned. 'A skiing injury? Doesn't quite fit in with a penniless vagrant, does it, Alex?' She turned the full gaze of her green eyes on him.

For a moment he simply looked at her. Then he shook himself and focused on her question. 'Anyone can become homeless, Martha,' he pointed out reasonably. 'And for some it becomes a way of life.'

'There was a plate?'

Randall nodded. 'With an ID number,' he said.

'So we can trace it back.'

'Hopefully. Mark Sullivan also thought that the operation had been done abroad. Apparently that prosthesis is not used in this country, which is why he thought about a skiing injury.'

Martha nodded. 'A shaft of femur then?'

'Yes.' Randall continued, 'He thought our man might have had a limp.'

'Oh dear.' Somehow it made the murdered man even more pathetic. Homeless, penniless, dirty and with a limp.

Randall continued, 'And there was a wrist injury that had happened round about the same time.' He frowned as he struggled to remember the name.

Martha supplied it. 'Scaphoid?'

'That's it.' Randall grinned at her.

'Age?'

'About forty-five. Mark couldn't be more precise than that.'

'And no one's come forward in response to your press coverage to say they knew him?'

'Nope. Nothing so far. It's early days yet. We've got officers looking at all the homeless haunts and talking to other vagrants but so far no one appears to know who he is or, more importantly from our point of view, who might have murdered him.'

Martha nodded. 'And if we can't find out his identity he'll have to be buried in an unmarked grave.'

'Courtesy of the council,' Alex agreed. 'But with the evidence of the prosthesis I'm confident we'll find out who he was,' Alex said. He frowned. 'What I mean is who he was before he joined forces with the vagrants, the shifting population. And finding out his identity, will that lead us to his killer?'

'It might do unless it was just a random assault by someone who hates vagrants,' Martha suggested.

Alex Randall eyed her thoughtfully. 'I suppose I prefer the former. The idea of a random murder on a homeless person fills me with foreboding. We could have assaults on all our street people.'

Martha was silent for a moment, then she met Randall's eyes with concern. 'You can't protect them all, can you?'

Randall shook his head, feeling the swamp of depression that accompanied the idea.

'I suppose your man's fingerprints weren't on your database?'

'No such luck. We got plenty of muck from under his nails but so far no skin, blood or anything else that might give us a clue as to his killer.' He looked across at her ruefully. 'Just dirt.'

She looked at him. Alex Randall was not a handsome man. In his forties with greying hair and a creased forehead, a thin, angular face and a tall, gangly figure, there was always something slightly hunted about him. Martha regarded him and wondered why he habitually wore that cloak of sadness, as though something in his life was holding back that boundless energy which radiated from his bony frame. She gave him a tentative smile, meant to encourage him to a confidence. Only a few years ago they had been comparative strangers.

And now?

He had become part of her life. She couldn't imagine life without him, or working with anyone else in that particular position.

'Are you sure he *was* a homeless man?'

'Going by his clothing and general air of

neglect I would think so,' he said cautiously. 'Also three days after his murder and in spite of intense media coverage no one has reported him missing, which indicates someone peripatetic. Rootless. A loner.' He paused, but now he was so well used to confiding in her it seemed easy. Natural. 'I am bothered by the fact that no possessions were found with him or near him. Absolutely nothing. No belongings.' He frowned. 'They all carry something. They have nowhere safe to leave their belongings so everything travels with them. But this guy . . . Nothing. No ID. Except this.'

He drew out the evidence bag containing the ancient child's leather shoe.

'What's that?'

'The only thing he appeared to carry with him. It was actually stitched into the lining of his coat.'

'But it looks ancient,' Martha pointed out. 'What was he doing with it?'

DI Alex Randall shrugged. 'I have absolutely no idea.'

Martha touched the bag thoughtfully. 'A talisman?'

'Again, Martha, I have no idea.'

'Weird,' she said. 'I think I read somewhere that putting a shoe in the chimney breast stopped the witches from coming down.'

Randall smiled. 'So what's the connection? You think he went to Moreton Corbet protecting himself from witchcraft with an old shoe?'

She smiled back. 'Not really.'

There was a pause.

'So, Alex, where do you go from here?'

'The usual, keep digging,' he said, then, getting up, 'I'd better be going.'

She stood up too, walked with him to the door. 'Keep me informed, Alex.'

It seemed to touch something in him. He grinned, looked happy. 'Do I ever not?'

And he was gone, leaving her to continue with her reflections.

Twelve

Sukey was home and as always she filled the house with her presence. Everyone and everything seemed more colourful and exciting when she was around. Even Vera, the daily (or more literally two-mornings-a-week) cleaner seemed snapped out of her usual curmudgeonly approach to life and smiled when Sukey began to dance her round the kitchen, singing some excerpts from the musical she was due to feature in. Martha watched her, beautiful, slim and leggy, her blonde hair flying around contrasting with Vera's stiffly permed grey locks, arthritic-like movements and stumpy legs. One thing that had always impressed Martha was the fact that though her daughter had never doubted that she would be an actress, she had never been pretentious enough to put the adjective *great* in front. Just to be an actress appeared to be enough for her. She had no pretensions.

Every corner in the house seemed to tingle with awareness of her daughter – the entire White House vibrant as though it was humming. She reached every corner, her voice, her belongings, her clothes strewn around the place, the scent of her perfume which followed her through the rooms, the sound of her music wafting round the house, light, quick steps everywhere, because Sukey was one of those women who never did anything slowly and because of her lightning speed she seemed to be in more than one place at a time. And yet she was elusive. One was always a couple of steps behind her, her scent the only hint that she had just passed through. Except in the kitchen, where her presence was solid and tangible. Food was very important to her so the scent and sound of cooking drew her to it like a bee to nectar. For a young woman with a very slim frame she was capable of eating very healthily. No anorexia for her. She wolfed down her meals but she was particular of the ingredients and would sit, thoughtfully chewing, making comments.

'I think a bit stronger cheese on the topping, Mum.' Or sometimes, 'This is nice. This is really, really nice,' which made Martha feel the trouble had all been worth it. She might be a coroner but her happiest role was simply being mother. However, as Martin had died so young, leaving her with twin toddlers, she had no option but to be the breadwinner. Whatever her own personal desires she had had to sweep them aside to work and support her family.

This was her life. And she wasn't complaining.

Even Bobby, who was getting on in years, bounced around Sukey like a puppy, wagging his tail non-stop, his tongue hanging out for walk after walk. Both twins were more than happy to oblige.

And as for Sam, he too looked happy to have his twin sister around again, even if it was only temporarily. There was no sight Martha loved more than seeing Sam's reddish hair bent over

Sukey's long blonde locks while they shared confidences. There was another reason for Sam's lift in spirits. He had confided in Martha that he was *having a chat* with the manager and the manager's mate, someone called Jack Arrowsmith, and they'd been *pretty encouraging* about his plans to resume his studies.

'Good,' she'd responded. 'That's good.'

Martha loved it. She had her family back – for now.

There was another reason why her own spirits soared. She was getting an inkling that the family, rather than shrinking, leaving her alone in the empty nest of the White House, might, at some time in the future, do the opposite and expand. Sukey now had a boyfriend, a nineteen-year-old called William Friedman who was the diametric opposite of her. Studious, introverted and quiet, he used his eyes a lot, watching everything and saying little. Martha wasn't too sure about him but he adored her daughter, was polite to her and seemed to get on OK with Sam.

Sam, who was making life-changing decisions. And even he was apparently not quite immune to the opposite sex. He'd said, in his gruff voice, during one of their early morning chats, that his friend's sister, someone called Rosalee, *wasn't too bad.*

And as if that wasn't enough of a clue, the look he had given her had been distinctly enquiring. She knew that look. He was searching for her approval.

Thirteen

It was PC Lara Tinsley who communicated the news to Randall. She found him bent over the computer screen. He was looking for similar assaults on homeless people in the last few years. Apart from the fatal assault on Joseph Gallagher there had been two other attacks on tramps but they had both been in the south of England – one in London three years ago and the other six months ago in Bournemouth.

In spite of himself, Randall felt amused at the location. He'd always thought of Bournemouth as the home of gentle, retired folk, not somewhere where they went tramp-bashing. Obviously nowhere was immune from prejudice. But Bournemouth? However, the only similarity in the three crimes was that the two other victims were also vagrants. All the assaults had been beatings with fists and feet. The crimes had been committed late at night, alcohol fuelled and in full view of well-placed CCTV. They did not have the subtlety or the cruelty of the murder of The Man; neither had had their throats cut and both had survived, though the London victim had died two months later, his injuries almost certainly a major contributory factor. The perpetrator in

96

that case was still in prison appealing against the charge of manslaughter, while the other had been convicted of GBH and was also still in prison. Randall sat still and thought. The police are very sensitive to the MO of a crime and these three cases (including the Shrewsbury assault) were inherently different. They could not help solve this case. There was one other glaring difference. The three previous assaults on the homeless had all taken place in town centres. The assault in Moreton Corbet was something different. A secretive, rural location well away from CCTV, bright street lights and witnesses.

He looked up as Lara entered his office space. Two years ago the force had gone open plan which was good in one way, for communication, but not so good for privacy. It was very difficult to have any sort of private conversation whether in person or over the phone. News or scandal swept around the office like an Australian forest fire in the height of summer.

'Sir,' PC Tinsley said tentatively. He looked up, met the big cow-brown eyes set in a face that even her best friend would only have described as pancake plain: a turned-up nose and small mouth.

'Yes?'

'We've had news from the forensic lab looking at our man's clothes.'

She fidgeted and Randall instinctively knew why. She wanted to call their victim something. Not just *The Man*. And not *John Doe*, which was clichéd and suggested no real identity at all, but someone whom they were content to remain forever anonymous. She wanted him to have a name. Dignity. Identity. He warmed to her and smiled at the diffident PC.

'And?' he prompted gently.

'They found something weird stitched into the bottom of the coat pocket wrapped up in a handkerchief.'

His eyebrows formed the question.

'They appear to be war medals, sir. Four of them.'

He could not have been more surprised. 'War medals?'

'Yes, sir. We believe they're Second World War medals.'

He felt his hopes rise. 'Is there a name on them?'

'Apparently not, sir.'

Randall sat silent, rolling his pen between his fingers. Cases were all like this, he reflected. Peaks and troughs like those formed by waves in a choppy sea. One minute you were on the crest, looking down, and the next plunged into murky depths, looking up.

Again, a clue as to the man's identity but, like the ancient child's shoe, this didn't make much sense either. Randall did some swift calculations. The Man was estimated to be around forty-five years old. That would mean he would have been born around 1970. His father may have been born in 1940 or even 1950 – still too young to have served for His Majesty in WWII. His grandfather then? Had this anonymous man taken the trouble to stitch his *grandfather's* medals into his trousers when he travelled so light? What on earth was all this about? A child's shoe from more than a hundred years ago and war medals about seventy years old?

He looked at the PC, bemused. 'Tinsley,' he said, 'take that shoe up to the museum, will you, see if you can get it dated and we'll take it from there. And we'll get someone else to examine the war medals and see if we can get some clue as to who . . .' he hesitated, '. . . this gentleman is.'

Or why he carried these two apparently unrelated objects.

'Yes, sir.'

'And have we circulated his dental records to the dentists?'

'I'll check, sir.'

'I think we'll talk again to the local press. I'll speak to the coroner – see if we can leak out a few more facts. We'll need to open and adjourn an inquest. Can you get a press meeting sorted out for later today?'

'Yes, sir.'

'Time we went public, don't you think?'

'Yes, sir.'

'And then at nine we'd better have another briefing.'

Tinsley tried to hide her dismay. A nine p.m. briefing meant another late night, which her husband would not appreciate. He would resent her 'devotion to the force' superseding her devotion to him. Greg Tinsley had his own cruel ways of showing his disapproval of his wife's career, which he interpreted as a dangerous independence. And there was always another willing woman to provide diversion and compound the punishment. He was a good-looking hunk or thug of a man, depending on your point of view.

Randall watched her go. He knew a little of her home life, of her husband's infidelity which had left her nervous and unhappy. He'd seen her wince at the late hour of their briefing, but he had a case to solve and all his officers deserved equal consideration for their home circumstances. He couldn't send her home at five o'clock every afternoon just because her husband was a philanderer any more than he could send Talith home to be with his pregnant wife or Roberts home to make whatever it was up with Flora, his girlfriend. Randall missed little of his officers' changing lives.

When PC Tinsley had drifted off with her list of tasks and instructions, Randall was left wondering. What if the medals and the shoe were nothing at all to do with the man and they were reading too much into them? What if he'd just found them somewhere, maybe in a skip or on a rubbish dump or something and they'd taken his fancy? He'd just pinched them, maybe not even going to sell them? Second World War medals probably had little value anyway. Had he stitched them into his coat purely to stop others from stealing them? But what if none of this led them to discover the man's identity?

Ever?

Then they would have to bury him, anonymous and in an unmarked grave.

It was something Alex Randall did not want to have to do.

Fourteen

Wednesday, 17 September, 1.30 p.m.

PC Tinsley pulled up outside Shrewsbury Museum, the shoe safely in her evidence bag. She'd looked at it on the way over – it was a strange piece of footwear, a worn wooden sole, almost like a clog. She could imagine a child clattering over cobbles in something like the Hovis advert. It had yielded little forensic evidence, which wasn't surprising. It must be a hundred years since it had been worn.

She parked up. She was to meet a young lady named Cindy Lopez who was apparently their best bet for information, and she had agreed to meet her here. Earlier on in the year Shrewsbury Museum had moved from Rowley Hall, a lovely half-timbered building near the Welsh bridge to the Music Hall, another interesting building, in the centre of the town near the old Market Hall in the square. Lopez was a small, stocky woman somewhere in her forties with unmistakably Spanish origins and a pleasant, effusive manner. She seemed eager to help and once they were in her office held out her hand for the evidence bag and spent some time studying its contents closely before she pronounced judgement.

'Turn of the last century,' she said decisively. 'At a guess, round about 1900.' She peered even closer and looked pleased. 'The sole . . .' she fingered it, '. . . is probably elder.' She looked up. 'Popular in Wales and the West Country.'

Tinsley squirrelled the fact away.

Cindy Lopes rattled on. 'For instance,' she said, 'the yew tree is symbolic of transformation, death and regeneration.'

Tinsley stared. Transformation, death and regeneration. The phrase had hit home. She couldn't have put it better herself. A man who had once enjoyed skiing and had had an accident had decided to go underground, for whatever reason. How better to describe this process than as being one of transformation and regeneration? He had transformed himself from a person who could afford skiing holidays to a homeless wanderer.

'Really?' she said, intrigued.

Cindy Lopez nodded. 'And represents exorcism, prosperity, banishment and healing. I could go on.'

And I could carry on listening, Tinsley thought, *but I don't think any of this is getting us answers.* So she gave the curator a polite smile and Cindy Lopez took the hint.

She fingered the bag. 'I wonder where this has been kept?' Her dark eyes fixed on Tinsley's. 'It's in remarkably good condition.' She looked at the PC. 'Nothing to do with that poor man who was found dead at Moreton Corbet Castle?'

'I'm sorry,' Tinsley said awkwardly.

'I know,' Cindy replied in a sing-song voice, mocking her a little. 'You're not at liberty to divulge.'

PC Lara Tinsley gave her a beatific smile.

Lopez focused back on the shoe. 'Well, I suppose I can help you a bit more. I don't think the shoe has been buried – the leather would have rotted and the sole wouldn't be in such good condition.'

'Can you tell me anything about where the shoe might have been made?'

Lopez gave her a sceptical look. 'You are grabbing at straws, aren't you?' she asked perceptively.

'Perhaps from the leather?' Tinsley asked hopefully.

Lopez shrugged. 'It is just ordinary cow leather,' she said.

'Or from the nails?'

'Again, these are handmade iron tacks. They used the same method all over the country – even abroad – like the Dutch clog.'

'Then the wood the sole is made from . . . perhaps? Didn't you say Wales or the West Country?'

'Yes, but not exclusively. Elders grow anywhere – near a stream.' Cindy Lopez peered at her then took out a magnifying glass to look even closer. 'There are certain regional differences in the wood they used for the sole of a clog but you can't be absolutely certain. They'd use whatever was available.' She examined the shoe more carefully.

And then Lopez made the most obvious of observations. 'Although this shoe would have belonged to a child of humble origins there is very little sign of wear, which is surprising. Shoes were handed from child to child. They weren't fussy about sizing correctly and boys and girls wore the same footwear. If there had been no use for the shoes they would have been sold. Money was tight, conditions harsh. And . . .' She looked up. 'Though it's been well and probably carefully preserved, you only have one shoe. We don't have its partner.'

Tinsley felt her head spin. Half a pair? Where was its partner? Over a hundred years old, not terribly well worn. Had the child only had one leg? Their tramp had had a limp. Was there a connection there? Or had the child died and the shoe been preserved as a keepsake? One shoe would be of no use to other children. Did this have any actual bearing on their case? How much could you glean from one small child's shoe over one hundred years old?

Cindy Lopez's other observations were more musings. 'Not a dainty little lady's shoe but a country child who walks through mud. A clod hopper, I think, is the phrase you use here,' she said, a bright twinkle in her dark eyes, 'and I suppose that it would have belonged to a little girl or boy about six. A sweet little child.' She lifted her eyebrows but Tinsley remained silent. Following her husband's spell of infidelity she had been thrilled to find herself pregnant and dismayed when only three short, happy, anticipatory, blissful weeks later, she had lost it. Since then – nothing. She sighed.

A sweet little child? Not, it seemed, for her.

Ms Lopez appeared not to notice.

A thought struck Lara Tinsley. 'You haven't

104

had a shoe like this one stolen from the museum, have you?'

'No. Our stuff here is mainly Roman and Celtic.'

'Is there a museum around here that has had a shoe like this stolen?'

'Not that I've heard. There's Blists Hill. They might have a little shoe like this in their collection but I haven't heard of one being stolen. If they have quantities of costumes I suppose it's possible that your gentleman just pinched it and they haven't noticed.'

Gentleman, Tinsley thought. She liked him being called a gentleman.

'But surely . . .' the curator queried, '. . . why? Why would he steal it? It's practically valueless. And it's hardly an object of beauty, is it?'

And that, Tinsley thought, was just another question. She proffered only one explanation. 'Maybe,' she said, 'it reminded him of a child – possibly his own.'

Lopez looked unimpressed and she was starting to lose interest. 'And I suppose you're not going to tell me a few more snippets about the background?'

'Sorry.' Tinsley tried not to sound rude but she had no wish to leak any more of the story to Cindy.

Besides which, what did they know? They were still at the asking questions stage.

Fifteen

Wednesday, 17 September, 3 p.m.

It was later that day that the first of their quests
bore fruit. A lorry driver arrived at the station
early in the afternoon. He was a big man, drawn
in, it seemed, by the boards placed at the side of
the A53 Shrewsbury to Market Drayton road via
Hodnet. His name, he said awkwardly, was
Nelson Futura, and he was a driver for a cattle
feed company. He delivered to farms.

He was overweight with a beer gut the size of
an eight-month pregnancy and was obviously
uncomfortable at finding himself at the police
station. He kept looking around him and fiddling
with the waistband of his jeans, which lay beneath
his swelling gut.

'I've come,' he said awkwardly, 'in response
to the boards you've put out on the road about
the tramp. You see, I think I might have picked
him up.'

Sandy Mucklow looked at him excitedly. 'Last
Thursday?'

Futura nodded.

'Between Shrewsbury and Moreton Corbet?'

'I had a delivery, see.'

Mucklow nodded.

'Some animal feed at the farm opposite the
castle,' he said. 'It were a filthy night but the rain

106

had stopped for just a bit. I saw this poor man at the side of the road and I thought it was about to chuck it down again. And I thought, why not? My employers,' he said, 'would go ballistic at me. I'm not supposed to pick up hitch-hikers but the sky was threatening thunder.'

Mucklow held his hand up. 'Just hang on there a minute,' he said. 'I'll fetch the senior investigating officer and you can make a statement.'

Nelson Futura looked troubled. 'My employers don't have to know, do they? I'll get the sack for sure.'

Mucklow shook his head. 'I don't see why they'd have to know,' he said. But already he could see a problem with this. They would have to check the driver's cab for any sign of trouble. But they could cross that bridge when they got to it.

Randall faced the driver across the interview table. He looked an honest man and a troubled one too. Mucklow had filled him in with the work conditions and he'd promised to see if he could keep this angle a secret.

'Where did you pick him up?'

'Just on the outskirts of the town. Just after the roundabout by the Two Henrys.'

So their man had already selected that road?

'He was already on the A53?'

Futura nodded.

'Have you ever seen him before?'

'No. And I wouldn't normally pick up a tramp,' Futura said frankly. 'They smell. But there was something about this man. He did look like one

107

of the great unwashed but he was dragging his leg.'

Randall felt a little skip at this statement. They knew something else about their man now. Mark Sullivan had been right. Their man's old skiing injury had resulted in a limp.

'And besides,' Futura continued, more comfortable now, 'it was about to chuck it down. He wouldn't want to get caught out in that.'

'So . . .?' Randall was thinking quickly. 'You were heading for . . .?'

'Moreton Corbet Farm,' Futura said.

'What time was this?'

'Just after five in the afternoon.'

'Did you know where he was heading?'

'No. I asked him if he wanted to be set down on the main road and he said no, he was heading for Moreton Corbet himself. I made a joke . . .' Futura looked proud of himself. 'I said it was fortuitous.'

Randall looked at him. One day, many moons ago, someone had used this word, fortuitous, to Nelson Futura and he had savoured it, remembered it, waiting for an opportunity to use it. And now he had finally aired it.

'Is there anything else you can tell us about the man? Did he seem fearful? Worried that somebody was looking for him? Did he mention any family, friends?'

Bemused Nelson Futura shook his head vigorously.

'Where did you drop him off?'

'I turned into the farm and said that was as far as I was going. I knew Mr Sharp wouldn't want

108

to see the likes of him around so I told him he'd better get out and go wherever it was that he was going. He thanked me for the lift and off he went.'

'Did Mr Sharp see the man leave your lorry?'

'I don't know. I couldn't be sure either way whether he saw him or not.'

'Was the gentleman carrying anything?'

Futura shook his head. 'Not that I saw but then he had that big thick coat on. He could have hidden anything under that.'

'Quite. OK. We'll need to take a quick look round the cab of your lorry.'

'That's all right.'

Randall frowned. 'Is there anything else you want to add?'

Futura shook his head. 'I reckon,' he said, 'I was the last person to see him alive.

Not quite, Randall thought. *Not quite.*

Sixteen

They found nothing obvious in Nelson Futura's lorry and let him go, but Randall resolved to check out whether Sharp had seen their man as he had climbed out of the cab.

PC Gary Coleman, in the meantime, was having a whale of a time on the internet. He was always happiest sitting in front of a screen anyway, asking it questions and evaluating the results, fingers flying over keys. He loved the feeling of all those facts literally at his fingertips. At the moment he was searching for some information on the medals that they had found stitched into their man's overcoat, and later he had arranged to meet up with an ex-serviceman in Oswestry to see if he could find out a little more about them. The serviceman's name was Mark Loftus and Coleman had tracked him down through the local branch of the ex-serviceman's club. He'd supplied the club with a sketchy background, that the medals had been found on a so far unidentified body, and they had recommended Major Loftus.

'Bit of an anorak,' they'd said, 'but if anyone can shed some light on your Second World War medals, it'll be him.'

Coleman had thanked them and arranged to meet up with him.

* * *

Mark Loftus, retired major, turned out to be in his nineties, with piercing blue eyes, a loud voice and still with an upright military bearing. Coleman almost expected him to salute as he approached him. But almost before he'd introduced himself he realized that the retired Major Loftus had all his mental faculties, a wonderful memory, an excellent power of recall and very good eyesight. He was a credit to the ninety-plus club. They met at the clubhouse, a little shabby these days, but the same could not be said of Major Loftus. He was up to scratch in a navy blue jacket, which now hung a little loose and grey trousers, a blue shirt and regimental tie with well-polished lace-up shoes, and greeted him with a bone-cracking handshake. On his left pocket also hung a pin with four medals attached.

'How do you do,' he said. 'Mark Loftus. Ex-King's Shropshire Light Infantry.' A smile crossed his face. 'Disbanded now and numbers dwindling. Only a few of us left sadly.' He spoke in a staccato tone, like the rat-tat-tat of gunfire.

Coleman mumbled something about him looking great for his age and the ex-soldier grunted, satisfied, and sat himself down. 'Don't do too badly,' he admitted. 'Sheltered accommodation, you know. They keep an eye on me.'

Coleman smiled and said he still thought he looked very well. The old chap brightened up at that. 'Mustn't grumble,' he said cheerfully. 'Now, what was it you wanted to know?'

Coleman showed him the four medals with their various ribbons. Three were copper-coloured and star shaped. The fourth was silver and the size of an old crown or five shilling piece. Coleman's grandfather had proudly presented him with a 1953 Coronation boxed crown when he had been sixteen years old so he recognized the size. Each of the ribbons was differently coloured. Gary Coleman knew a little about them from the internet but what he could not do was deduce anything from the collection. This was what he hoped Major Loftus would be able to help him with.

Loftus went first to the medal on the right, the silver crown-sized one. 'This,' he said, 'is the War Medal, sometimes erroneously known as the Victory Medal.' The blue eyes skewered the policeman as though to scold him. 'That,' he said severely, 'is quite incorrect.'

Coleman nodded and the ex-serviceman continued with his explanation.

'It was awarded to those who served in the Armed Forces or Merchant Navy for at least twenty-eight days between the third of September 1939 and second of September 1945.'

Coleman thought that this medal would have been given to an awful lot of servicemen and asked him if it had.

It provoked quite a response. 'Good gracious me, yes. Thousands.'

Hardly narrowed the field then.

Major Loftus continued, unaware of the policeman's disappointment. 'The second one . . .' He moved to the one to its left, one of the copper-coloured stars. 'The Atlantic Star,' he said, 'awarded for six months' service afloat.'

Coleman's pulse quickened. *Afloat.* That, surely,

112

narrowed the field? He looked expectantly at the old soldier.

'The next one is the Italy Star, another campaign medal in Italy, Greece, Yugoslavia and so on. Your man,' he said, looking up, 'had quite a war.'

But he wasn't his man. He was The Man who couldn't possibly have gained all these medals in the war. He hadn't been born until twenty-five years after the Armistice had been declared.

'And the last?' Coleman asked, trying not to let his chagrin show.

'Another Campaign medal. Known as the 1939–1945 Star.' He looked at the pin thought-fully. 'I suspect,' he said, 'that your man was a merchant seaman.'

'He isn't exactly *my* man,' Coleman said awkwardly, 'and he can't have served in the war at all. The deceased is only in his mid-forties.'

Loftus thought for a moment about this before barking, 'Not even his father then.' He frowned. 'I wonder how many grandchildren hang on to their *grandfather's* old medals.' He gave Coleman another piercing glare. 'I bet mine won't. These things . . .' his eyes moved over the strip of medals with real sadness, '. . . come up for sale in their numbers these days on the internet and that eBay thing. My niece told me the other day that there were even a couple of Victoria Crosses on there. Disgraceful, I call it.' It was said with real feeling. 'These fellows gave up their lives, their loves, their futures. And does anyone care?'

Coleman was at a loss for words.

The old soldier gave another heartfelt sigh and Coleman carried on. 'Would it be possible,' he asked slowly, 'for a search to narrow it down to a specific officer? You see, we don't know who this man is – was. It would help to at least know who he was. There isn't a name engraved on these?'

'No. For some reason no names were engraved unless you were Canadian or Indian and I think the South African and Aussies had their names on too, but not our boys. There were too many of them.' The old soldier went into reminiscent mode again. 'Too – bloody – many,' he said. 'Young, fit.' He stopped himself from a second rant and said instead, 'Bloody awful thing, war, Constable.'

Coleman nodded. He'd always thought so.

He rose to go and the old soldier rose too in a dignified, polite gesture, getting to his feet stiffly and slowly. Coleman shook his hand and thanked him for his help and Loftus, retired major, haw-hawed. 'Glad to be of assistance,' he said. 'Wouldn't want the world to forget.'

Lest we forget. It was the phrase, along with *the going down of the sun*, that best evoked an old soldier. War poetry, some of the most terrible and beautiful words. Coleman was in a reflective mood as he drove back to Shrewsbury, and vowed to put a tenner in the poppy tin in November.

Seventeen

The press conference was well attended, journalists still filing in at six o'clock, the official starting time. Perhaps it was the dramatic backdrop of Moreton Corbet Castle alongside the bloodthirsty image of an unknown tramp with his throat cut that made such good copy.

Randall looked around the room – standing room only – and wondered who was responsible for some of the more lurid headlines.

Homeless man found in tragic ruin.

Who is this man? An artist's impression followed below.

Cut throat at the castle. He'd winced at that one.

Bloodbath in twelfth-century ruin. Not exactly!

Murder at Moreton Corbet Castle. Well, at least that was factually correct.

The curse of the castle. Sounded almost Shakespearian.

He made a face and knew he could never have been a journalist. What would they make of his story? he wondered, and quickly shut this question down in his mind.

Interestingly, the papers had chosen to feature not only the instantly recognizable facade of the ruin but also had printed a potted history of the place. Moreton Corbet Castle was now famous suddenly for housing a Royalist Civil War sympathiser. After four hundred years?

Randall could never quite understand how things captured the public imagination.

They'd even dredged up Holmyard's ancient curse – the curse, as legend had it, that after the bombardment of the Parliamentarians the castle would never be completed. And looking at the house one could see that curse or not this had come true. It was and always had been unfinished.

All these dramatic headlines and scurrilous stories had made the police's job harder. They had brought the general public day-tripping out to the area in their numbers. And the road system simply could not cope. The personnel manning the forensic van had reported increased problems with traffic, so they'd shut one or two of the narrower country lanes and restricted access. Randall gave a cynical smile as he surveyed the journalists. He had always thought that the press made a great servant but an unpredictable leviathan of a master. One could not control it. Particularly in these days of tweets and instantly accessible news supplied by the internet. Not just the internet sat in front of your computer safely connected at home but anywhere, anytime or any place on your 4G smartphone or tablet. The general public as well as the newspapers, TV and radio would be always be drawn to a dramatic place with a dramatic story, however tackily it was presented. And yet, he thought as he scanned the full room, so far, even with the full exposure they still did not know who their man was.

No one, it seemed, could tell them his name. The most simple fact of all. And as for finding out the perpetrator, they were nowhere near.

Randall pinned both the artist's impression and the man's picture, taken before the post-mortem, on the board and the room stilled.

He began with the bare bones, the approximate age of the murdered man, using a plan of the area around the ruin to indicate where the body had been found. Then he released some forensic detail: the blood spattering and lividity, giving a brief explanation of post-mortem pooling of the blood for the hacks, though he knew full well that hardened crime correspondents would know exactly what lividity was and its significance. The body had not been moved after death. He also told them the findings of the post-mortem: the old injuries to the leg and wrist.

The detail about the shoe and the medals he kept back until later on in the meeting.

He drew their attention to the leg. 'It was the right leg,' he said. 'A fractured shaft of femur, that's the large thigh bone, which had been repaired with a pin and plate. We believe the injury was done sometime in the nineties, and was probably repaired abroad.'

Immediately a hand shot up.

He recognized her. Jennifer Purloin, intelligent representative of the *Metro*, the London freebie. 'How can you know, sir, that it was repaired abroad?'

Good question. He nodded approvingly. 'The

prosthesis is of a type that is not used over here.' He hesitated. 'The pathologist told us that it had a bad track record . . .' He was on shaky ground here, struggling to recall precisely what Mark Sullivan had told him. 'There are more complications with this prosthesis than the one we use in the UK. The significance of this is that it resulted in a limp. We now know this is so.'

They started scribbling and Randall continued, 'We are working on an assumption that the wrist injury and the leg injury were possibly the result of a skiing accident.'

More scribbling.

'We know now how our man arrived at his destination. He hitch-hiked a lift in a lorry which was going to Moreton Corbet, so it's quite possible that it was a coincidence that he was there and took shelter in the castle from the rain. His coat was dry.' He made a mental note to pursue the source of that coat as well as the trousers. He would send PC Shaw off on that one.

He continued. 'Our man had no possessions on him except . . . I'll come on to those later. He had no sleeping bag, which, if he had been sleeping rough, he would have needed. His fingerprints are not on our database.' To these hardened hacks he hardly needed to spell out what that meant.

'We have visited the various haunts . . .' He wished he hadn't needed to use the word but he repeated it, '. . . haunts,' pause, 'of the homeless and he has been recognized, but none of the people who had dealings with him when he was

118

alive are aware of either his name or his background.' As he spoke he realized how very unusual this was. Everyone has a name. Why had this man kept his secret in life as well as in death? He frowned. Could it be because it was a well-known name? Instantly recognizable?

He felt he should add something here. 'This is a particularly violent crime, which might have been premeditated. The assailant must have had a sharp knife on him.' The comment pricked Sullivan's phrase in him. Kitchen devil. Sullivan's words. 'We don't know whether this was a chance meeting or a coincidence. Other attacks in the area on vagrants have been different and we're working on the assumption that the crimes are not connected. We are naturally anxious to know the exact sequence of events and find out who committed this crime.' He'd done this before, involved the press in the intellectual solving of a crime, coaching them to ask the questions the police themselves ask.

To rope them in he threw questions out into the room.

'Was the motive possibly theft? Unlikely. Perhaps a personal resentment against homeless people? Was it a sudden outburst of rage at finding the man there and our assailant just happened to have the knife? Is it possible that our man was the one carrying the knife, possibly as protection? We don't know. What we do know is that in his possession were two objects.' He indicated the PowerPoint pictures. 'This, which appears to be a Victorian child's shoe or clog. Its age is estimated by Shrewsbury Museum as being around

1900 and, judging by the size, was probably worn by a child of around six.' He looked at it, knowing there was something there which he should be registering. What was it? It had been described as a country child's shoe. What was the phrase the woman had used? Clod hopper. And then he knew what it was. This shoe never had hopped through clods. It was hardly worn.

And that was it.

He realized the newspaper people were watching him curiously, waiting for him to continue.

'Did he find it somewhere and keep it, possibly as a trophy? Is it possible he stole it?'

He hardly knew whether to say this and almost dreaded reading the papers in the morning. 'All sorts of theories have been put forward. Is there some significance in the object? It has even been put forward that a shoe could be used as a talisman against witchcraft or evil. Is that why he carried it?'

The entire room simply gawped at him.

Good, Randall thought. That is exactly the response he wanted. At least they weren't asleep.

'That wasn't the only strange object our man was carrying.'

He went on to the next picture showing all four medals, ribbons hanging on their pin, and saw an array of equally confused expressions.

He ran through each medal in turn, put forward the suggestion Major Loftus had made. Then pointed out that it was impossible that their victim had served in the Merchant Navy in the Second World War. 'Not only was he not born for another twenty-five years,' he said, 'but even his father would almost certainly have been below the age of enlistment at the time of the Second World War.'

The puzzlement on the faces compounded.

Join the club, Randall thought. *The club of utter confusion. The when, where, why, how, what and most frustratingly who club. Welcome to our ranks.*

'So if the medals were awarded to a family member,' Randall pointed out, 'it could only have been his grandfather – unless his father had been born in or before 1921, that is, and he had his son in his fifties. This is, of course, possible.'

Now the assembled journalists merely looked confused and Randall shared their sentiment.

With bells on.

He hurried on to a place where he was more sure of himself.

'We've circulated his dental records in the vain hope that this will help us identify our man but vagrants are not generally known to make regular attendances at dentists' surgeries.'

They had the decency to titter before Simone Dixon of the *Shrewsbury Chronicle* spoke up. 'You say have there been other similar assaults on homeless people? I believe one homeless man died recently in Shrewsbury as the result of an assault?' She looked down at her notebook. 'A Mr Joseph Gallagher.'

'The two crimes are so dissimilar,' Randall said tightly, 'that we do not think there is a link.' He felt he should say more. 'There have been, it is true, drunken fisticuffs. There have been two deaths of vagrants both as a result of assault, one here and the other in London, who died two months later, almost certainly as a result of the assault. But there has been nothing as violent and premeditated as this.'

She seemed to accept this. 'Thank you, sir.'

Randall looked at Simone Dixon with interest. How old was she? Twenty – twenty-one? He just hoped she stayed here in the town. She was bright and good at her job. What was more, when he answered her question she listened to the answer, took notes and was quiet, accepting his explanation. He wouldn't mind a few more of those. Argumentative buggers, the press could be.

There were a few more questions from local and national journalists and Randall felt satisfied. They would do what they could to help find out who their man was and how, or rather why he had died and the more important question of who had killed him. Was there a reason? Was it connected to the objects their man had taken such care to retain? Or was there a possibility that the objects had been stitched into the coat by someone else?

The press conference disbanded at 6.20 p.m.

By nine the officers were gathered for the briefing. Randall cast his eyes over Lara Tinsley. She was calm and contained, her face bland and expressionless. She looked resolute and nodded an affirmative when he asked whether she had released the request for dentists to check their records. Dental records could be a great key but these days, with so many of the younger generation having perfect teeth or the older generation not being able to afford a dentist, they could be less helpful. Besides – as he had indicated in the press conference – he couldn't see their vagrant making an appointment for six monthly check-ups and scale and polishes. He didn't hold out much hope from this source.

Tinsley then fed back the result of her encounter with the curator of Shrewsbury Museum and Coleman shared with the rest of his colleagues the story of his encounter with Major Loftus.

This lightened the atmosphere and resulted in a few smiles and sniggers.

Not a bad thing, Randall thought. Tinsley and Coleman had given him the information about the shoe and the medals earlier, in time for the press conference.

The rest of the briefing consisted of running through known facts and Randall could tell that some of the initial excitement and drama was beginning to wear a bit thin. Part of his job as SIO was to keep morale up and the pace going. He focused on avenues of enquiry: neighbours, witnesses, charity shops, the nuns. There were plenty of questions to be asked but, so far, precious few answers. Randall knew that they had to wait for someone to make a connection between their man and his violent death.

When they had all left it was well gone ten but Randall felt fidgety. He picked up the phone. He had Martha's private number and she had once told him that he was welcome to use it at any time if he had a problem over a case. She had added, 'Or anything else.'

It was tempting. This was not exactly a problem over a case but he did want to talk. He glanced

at his watch, hesitating before dialling. It was
10.35 p.m. and it was too late to ring her. He
couldn't intrude on her life like this.

He put the phone down.

124

Eighteen

Thursday, 18 September, 8.20 a.m.

The press reports had borne fruit by early the next morning.

And this woman knew exactly how to report to the correct officer. She marched into the Monkmoor station and demanded to see the SIO.

Special Dean Kramer was manning the hatch. 'SIO?' he queried, confused.

'Senior – Investigating – Officer,' she spelled out slowly and patronizingly.

'Investigating . . .?' Kramer wasn't quite the brightest button in the box and he wasn't used to the general public being so familiar with police jargon.

The woman gave a loud sigh. 'The murder of the tramp,' she said uncompromisingly. 'The one who was found with his throat cut at Moreton Corbet.'

Kramer's eyes widened. 'Certainly. I'll get hold of Detective Inspector Randall for you, madam.'

The look she gave him was fearsome. He half expected her to tell him not to *madam* her but she contented herself with a harrumph of impatience accompanied by a glare and pacing around the waiting area while he fetched DI Randall.

He found him studying on the computer, trying

to piece it all together. Looking for something. Anything. He was getting desperate.

He looked up as Dean approached and frowned. He wasn't sure about him, whether he would make the grade or not. Still . . . one had to give the lad a chance.

'Sir,' Kramer said tentatively, 'there's a lady here wishing to speak to you – as SIO,' he added, his voice conveying the importance of the title.

Randall stood up and followed him down the corridor.

The woman was tall and very thin with a sharp, angular body that matched her sharp, angular face, her hair straight and grey, cut mannishly. Her eyes were ice blue and very shrewd. Randall greeted her courteously, introducing himself.

First, she checked his credentials. 'You're the detective in charge of this investigation of the murdered vagrant?'

'I am.'

'I knew him,' she said.

Immediately Randall's heart began to soar. She knew him? Their man? Alive?

'Perhaps it would be better,' he said, 'if we went somewhere quiet, somewhere where we can talk.' He could feel the hope bubbling up in his chest.

The woman nodded and Randall led her into one of the interview rooms. He offered her a cup of tea which she accepted and sat down, her back ramrod straight.

Randall began the interview, speaking gently. This was a woman who had come forward to

126

volunteer information. She might be the breakthrough they needed.

'My name,' she said, 'is Genevieve Dreyfuss. My father was French, my mother Welsh. I live in one of the cottages on Pontesbury Hill.'

She paused then gave him a severe look. 'That, of course, is irrelevant. As is the fact that I was the headmistress of a small boarding school in Gloucestershire. I moved here five years ago because I'd always liked Shrewsbury. My mother was fond of the place.'

Randall waited. She would get to the point soon, surely? He only hoped that the point was worth the preamble.

'Sorry,' she said. 'I do apologize.' Something like humour softened the severe features 'Wasting police time, I daresay. Hope you won't charge me, Inspector.'

He shook his head. She must have been a great head-mistress.

'Tell me what you know,' he prompted gently.

'He used to come and do some work in the garden for me,' she said. 'He knocked on the door one day and said he would do some weeding in return for a bowl of the delicious-smelling soup I was making. Parsnip and ginger,' she explained, then stopped. 'Another irrelevance. He had the most lovely voice, you know. Clear and gentle. Almost like an actor's.'

There was only one way he could answer this. 'I never heard him speak.'

When he had seen him the man's throat had been cut right through. No chance of him hearing that lovely voice.

She must have quickly realized her faux pas. She flushed. 'No. Oh, how awful. No, of course . . .' The polite response had flustered her. 'I'm so sorry,' she said again.

'His name?'

'He never gave me his name.' She paused. 'I had the impression that he deliberately avoided giving me his name.'

Disappointing. But Randall kept trying. 'His accent?'

'He was accentless. There was no clue there as to his background.'

'Did he tell you why he'd taken to the road?'

'No. He told me one day that the reason he'd disappeared was because he could.'

If Randall had deemed this case unfathomable this certainly didn't help. 'What do you think he meant by that?'

'He said it was because he was already dead.'

Randall leaned forward. 'What?'

'That's what he said. 'He was already dead.'

'Did he enlarge on that?'

'No. But I can tell you he was not an unintelligent man. He knew about gardening. He understood what to do, when to prune, how to prune, when to mulch, those sorts of things. And he had some skill. I believe that at one time he must have cared for his own garden.'

Randall couldn't think of anything to say in response but Genevieve Dreyfuss continued unabashed. 'Sometimes I'd hear him hum, usually an aria or song from some musical or opera.' She hesitated, met his eyes. 'He was a cultured man, Inspector.'

128

'Did you *ask* him his name?'

'I did. He said it wouldn't be of any use to me because his name was listed amongst those of the dead.'

Randall frowned. This man's name should have been Enigma. Why had he been so anxious for no one to know who he was? The thought crept into his mind. *Because when someone had found out who he was he had silenced him.* This put a new slant on the case. He looked back at Miss Dreyfuss, who was trying. He had to give her that.

'I did ask him what he meant by being classed as one of the dead, Inspector, but he simply smiled at me and said that he was happy to remain nameless, amongst the dead.'

Randall pictured the bank of fridges in the mortuary. Well, he'd got his wish. Their man certainly now was nameless and one of the dead.

If he had found this a baffling case from the start, Ms Dreyfuss's visit had, if anything, only added to his confusion. She was an intelligent woman. She had known the deceased. She must have formed her own opinion. He tried. 'What did *you* think he meant by that?'

She was silent, thoughtful. 'I suppose,' she said slowly, 'that I thought he meant that something had happened to him in the past and he had put that life behind him.' Shrewd eyes looked at him. 'People do use those terms, don't they? You know – if they've found Jesus or left some unpleasant situation. I wondered if he'd perhaps been to prison.'

Randall shook his head. 'We fingerprinted him,'

he said. 'Whoever he was and whatever had caused him to go underground, it wasn't because he'd committed a crime.'

'I'm glad,' she said sentimentally.

He felt he should apply pressure here. 'Miss Dreyfuss, so far in this investigation we have few people who knew our man alive. The nuns at the abbey, who didn't know him very well, the girls at McDonald's' – he made a mental note to chase this lead up – 'and the lorry driver who picked him up and drove him to Moreton Corbet, where he was murdered in the castle grounds. Apart from those few people you are the only person who has admitted to knowing this poor man alive.'

The statement appeared to stun her, almost to intimidate her. 'I did try and help him,' she repeated earnestly. 'I am now. I'm doing what I can.'

'Can you think of any reason why anyone would want to kill him?'

'No,' she said firmly. 'He was a thoroughly nice man.'

'Did he ever say anything to you about someone threatening him?'

Again, she shook her head.

'Did he mention *anything* about his past life?'

'Again, no.' She seemed to think an apology was needed and looked anguished. 'I'm so sorry. I'm not being much help here, am I?'

No, was the truth, but there was little point in focusing on that. Randall continued, 'To your knowledge, did you ever see him carry a knife?'

'No.'

She seemed startled by the question but he had to pursue this line. 'Was he a violent man, Miss Dreyfuss?'

This time she was affronted. 'Absolutely not.'

'In the paper did you see the picture of an old-fashioned child's shoe that he carried with him?'

She nodded.

'Have you ever seen that before?'

A slow, puzzled shake of the head. 'I never saw it.'

'And what about the war medals?'

This provoked a further shake of the head.

'Did he ever mention family?'

'Nothing.'

'Friends?'

Again, a negative.

'Any little clue? A date? A name? A place?'

'Nothing. I have thought about it, you know, gone over every moment he spent in my garden or eating at my table.'

Randall tried to prompt her memory. 'He had a limp.'

'It wasn't terribly noticeable. Only if he was tired, and I put it down to a stiff back after gardening.' Her face tightened as though recalling something. Randall was tempted to prompt her but instead he waited. 'He said it was due to an old injury.'

Yes? He didn't dare voice it.

'Skiing, he said. It was the only reference he ever made to his previous life and I remember it particularly because I was so surprised. I mean, one knows that most of these homeless people at one point did live somewhere, did have money, did have people around them who loved them but . . . skiing. Well, put it like this. It was a shock.'

Randall nodded. 'Do you think he might at one time have been a professional gardener?'

'I don't think so,' she said frowning.

'Did you have a guess as to his trade or profession?'

'No. He was handy with tools but he never said what work he had done.'

'Did he ever use a phrase that might have given you a clue as to his geographical origin?'

'No.'

'Or make any comment on, say, war or country, wealth, status, cars?'

'No.'

'What did you call him?' Randall asked curiously.

She smiled, embarrassed. '*Excuse me* or *please, sir* or . . . I never knew his name,' she insisted and Randall was flummoxed.

'I did tell him that my garden shed was always open. There was a sun lounger in there and a few old blankets. I told him that he could sleep in there if he ever felt the need. Any time.' Again, she seemed to feel that her treatment of him was open to criticism. 'He didn't want more,' she said. 'I'd give him money if he'd done some work for me and I would give him food. He was a nice man.' She looked upset. 'It is quite dreadful what happened to him.'

Randall felt a prick of interest. 'Did he leave any belongings in your shed?'

'He might have done. I never really looked.

Not carefully. He put the tools away quite neatly so I had no need to go in there.'

'And since you heard about his murder?'

'I only realized when I read this morning's headlines in the paper.'

'Which were?'

'"Hobo has throat cut,"' she said disapprovingly.

Randall winced.

'But the artist's picture was a very good likeness.'

It was true. Dane Banks, their police artist, had a real talent for portraits, but he could never have thought when he went to art college that he would end up reconstructing living faces from the dead or, even worse, from bones, colour in terrible facial injuries, replace missing eyes, noses, damaged mouths or be asked to age the disappeared so that ten or twenty years later their relatives and acquaintances might recognize them. Correctly or mistakenly.

Like the Tichborne claimant.

Randall continued his questions. 'How often did he come?'

'It was quite erratic – not regular at all. I never knew when to expect him, which is why I didn't miss him. Sometimes he'd come a couple of mornings in a week, at other times I wouldn't see him for a month or more.'

'Did he work for anyone else in the area?'

She shrugged. 'I really don't know, Inspector. Not that I know of.' Her manner changed to become haughty. 'I don't really mix with my neighbours.'

Randall covered a smile with a cough. 'How long has he been coming to your garden?'

'Three years or so.'

'Is there anything else you can think of that might help us find out who killed him?'

She looked blank. 'No.'

'*Anything* more?' he appealed. He still didn't have a handle on this mysterious man, though a little like one of Dane Banks's sketches, features were beginning to emerge.

'One thing I should say,' she said, getting up to leave, 'is that he was a man contented with his position.'

'Contented?' It was a shocking word to use, both in relation to his status and to his murder.

But the word didn't faze Genevieve Dreyfuss. 'Yes. He told me one day that he was lucky, that cats may have nine lives but most humans only had one. He told me he had already had two.'

More confused than ever, Randall gave her a card, asked her to ring him if she recalled anything else that might help their investigation and called an urgent briefing.

Once he'd brought everyone up to date with this latest development, he rang Martha.

Martha's morning was proving to be an odd one. She had had a long talk with a statistician who was looking at death rates and causes of death in various towns, cities, hospitals and nursing homes. While Shrewsbury's residents were, in fact, largely healthy, demographics showed that there was a propensity towards a more elderly population than in the national average and this

134

had a knock-on effect. It skewed the death statistics and she was finding it hard to work out where and how she should be collating this information. But it was necessary so they would have an early alert in the case of a repeated Dr Shipman who, though he had been the most evil of men, had, in a strange way, done the general public a service. He had stopped them having blind faith in their doctors. Never again. Faith – yes. Blind – no. Although she largely trusted the medical profession, being a member of it herself, she subscribed to the mantra: keep your eyes open and your wits about you.

Each month she had to submit facts and figures to the government body responsible for births, marriages and deaths – or hatch, match and dispatch as they were often called. The trouble was that computers could only accept information in straight lines and tidy boxes. They wanted cause of death 1, 2, 3, 4. A bit of this and a bit of that simply wasn't good enough. But the causes of death in the elderly were rarely clear cut. They might have been a bit of heart failure, a bit of pulmonary disease, diabetes, Alzheimer's, peripheral vascular disease and so on. At least, Martha reflected, staring out of the window at the spike of St Mary's Church, they now accepted old age as a valid cause of death. So heart failure due to old age due to . . .? She smiled.

In spite of her quandary, something inside her felt light and happy today, and when Jericho buzzed her at 12.30 p.m. to say that Detective Inspector Alex Randall wondered if he could have a word with her, she was almost floating.

'Alex.'

He stood in the doorway, simply staring at the lovely woman who was smiling the warmest smile he'd ever seen. He felt its radiant heat from right across the room. Her hair seemed like a flame against the sunshine which poured in through the window behind her. For a moment he could not speak, and for once he felt he did not need to.

Having let the detective in, Jericho closed the door, shaking his grey locks. Nothing good would come out of this friendship, he was sure.

Meanwhile, somewhere in the country a dentist was looking through his emails. Police frequently discover an identity through dental records. Maybe not this time?

'Not possible,' the dentist said, shaking his head as he pressed delete.

Nineteen

Martha's office had a formal, slightly sombre feel to it: mahogany bookshelves, a leather-topped mahogany desk, a large, bowed window which overlooked the town from afar, the spire of St Mary's standing like a trophy tower. Her vibrant colouring – a throwback to Celtic roots – Welsh father and Irish mother – was at odds with both her position and the formality of the room. As Randall stood just inside the door, that was his thought. And he suddenly felt he would rather be meeting her somewhere else, somewhere less formal, where they would be on an even footing and could talk about subjects other than murder and death.

She caught his hesitation and bit her lip, uncertain what to say. She took a step towards him. He caught a waft of Chanel No. 5 and smiled. Not quite the non-conformist then.

'Any news?' she asked. 'Have you found out who your man is yet?' She stopped herself. 'Or should I call him our man? He is our joint responsibility, Alex.'

He nodded. 'I need a walk,' he said, hardly realizing what he had just suggested. 'Can you play hooky for a while?'

Slowly she nodded, perfectly aware that this was quite a step, something very much other than work. 'It's a lovely day, Alex,' she said. 'Why don't we walk through The Quarry?'

137

The people of Shrewsbury were lucky enough to have their very own park right in the middle of town. Known as The Quarry, it contained an exquisite sunken garden planted by their ex-parks attendant – a man called Percy Thrower.

She gave Jericho a brief explanation of her departure and watched his face tighten in disapproval, but he said nothing.

And twenty minutes later, each clutching a Costa coffee, they found themselves on the wide path at the side of the sparkling Severn River, lime trees providing dappled shade, the waters shining silver, reflecting trees, the boat house and the Porthill footbridge, scene of many a school dare and responsible for two deaths that Martha had presided over. She shook herself. Must she connect everywhere with death, tragedy or felony?

They sat, like Derby & Joan, on the warm grass, not caring that it was slightly damp. And Alex Randall started unburdening himself about the case, telling her the latest development, describing the characterful woman who had told them all she knew about their tramp, that he had spent time living in her shed, that he'd dug her garden competently, that he had seemed to her to be cultured, that he appeared to have deliberately withheld his name for an unknown reason, as well as his cryptic phrases about having more than one life and being happy to remain nameless, amongst the dead. As he spoke he was aware that the murdered man was gradually being coloured in, coming to life, becoming a person, someone three-dimensional.

Moving, speaking, humming, living, working.

He looked at her. 'How can he have had two lives?'

'Well, it makes sense,' Martha said. 'In a way he *has* had two lives. His first as someone who went skiing, probably with family or friends, and the second as a lonely hobo. Two lives, Alex,' she said. 'Two lives.'

'Which ended with . . .' He didn't need to finish the sentence.

They were companionably silent then Martha touched his hand and looked at him earnestly. 'I hate it that he doesn't have a name, you know,' she said.

Randall met her eyes. 'Well, I don't like it, either,' he said. 'But what can we call him?'

'Charlie,' she said, lights flickering through her eyes. 'The tramp? Charlie Chaplin?'

He leaned back and in spite of himself he smiled. 'Not quite,' he said. 'Knowing what we do about him I don't think Charlie's quite right, do you? Charles,' he said. 'We shall call him Charles. It's as good a name as any, though it doesn't quite fit with the pretty ghastly injury we saw.'

'No,' she agreed gently, lying back now on the warm grass, her eyes shielded from the sun. 'It doesn't but it gives him a character; it makes him a person. Not just a crime . . .' she thought of her morning's work, '. . . and a statistic.'

Randall nodded, sitting up, his hands around his knees. 'But giving him a name doesn't provide us with answers, Martha,' he said, looking down at the slim figure in a dark blue dress, white sandals, her red hair spread on

139

green grass. 'We still don't know who he is, who killed him, why – if there is a reason – where he came from, why he elected to lose his identity and stay lost. And what about these strange statements he made, that he was "already dead" and had had two lives? It isn't just the violent crime,' he said thoughtfully. 'It's much more than that.'

'Yeah.'

They were momentarily quiet.

Then she sat up, remembering something, 'What about the number on the prosthesis? Any luck with that?'

'Not as much as we'd hoped. They used them in France, Switzerland, Spain and Germany. They're looking into identifying where it was inserted and who the patient was but it could take some time. It was a few years ago – their records weren't computerized then.'

In spite of herself, Martha smiled. 'What was life like before the instant access of Microsoft and Wikipedia?'

Randall smiled too. 'I can hardly remember. But anyway . . .' He met her eyes. 'I'm not holding my breath on that one.'

'You still have other avenues of enquiry?'

'Yes.' He spoke with a little more jollity than he felt.

Silence dropped between them heavy as a stone.

Martha wanted to ask him personal questions. Are you married? Do I mean anything to you other than as a colleague? Do you have children? Once he'd mentioned he'd *had a son*. Strange words, set in the past, full of implication, but he hadn't enlarged.

Why do you never talk about your family? Never mention wife, parents, brothers, sisters? Why do you wrap yourself up in the cloak of secrecy and anonymity, giving me only occasional glimpses of your vulnerability? Why do you look so sad sometimes?

As well as more general questions. Where do you live? What do you do with your leisure time? That, she decided, was the safest option and the only one she could ask.

She began with a laugh. 'What do you do when you're not at work, Alex? What hobbies do you have?'

'I like to walk,' he said, looking at her oddly, as though wondering why she was exploring this particular avenue.

'Do you have a dog then?' Safer than, *Do you have a wife?*

He laughed, still looking at her in that puzzled way. 'No. I like to walk – alone.' He paused. 'I like to think while I'm walking.'

'Any particular place? Near your home?' She tried to ask this airily, but the moment the words were out of her mouth she knew she'd failed.

He turned his perceptive hazel eyes on her. He knew exactly what this was. An interrogation.

She gave a tiny laugh and an even tinier smile, then sat up. 'Maybe we should . . .'

He gripped her arm. 'I'm married,' he said.

Her heart beat slowed. 'Oh,' was all she could say.

He was shaking his head and pulling at her arm now as though to physically stop her from thinking what she was thinking or from going. 'No,' he said. 'It isn't what you think.'

She looked at him. *Please, please don't give me the old chestnut that your wife doesn't understand you.*

She didn't need to say the words. He read them in her face and as a result chose his words even more carefully. 'My marriage is a miserable state of affairs,' he said.

Now she put a warning hand on his arm. *Do not spoil this. Don't make me think less of you.*

He knew exactly what she was thinking and looked away. He didn't want to see disappointment in her bright eyes. 'If you met my wife you would know instantly. Martha,' he said, desperation making his voice hoarse, 'I don't know whether she's mad or bad.'

And she was shocked. She looked at him, opened her mouth to speak and could not find a single word to respond in anyway remotely appropriate.

The trouble with being a single woman, a widow, is that you leave yourself wide open, vulnerable; you can too easily appear needy or standoffish, predatory or cold. None of these was how she wanted to appear.

But Alex Randall seemed to want nothing from her now. He was staring out across the river at the Boat House and the dog walkers and a rowing team sculling their way skilfully against the current. A beautiful sight, the entire team working as one, oars flashing in the bright September sun, their coxswain's orders floating across the water to them.

'*Pull. Left. Right. And* . . .'

'We had a son,' he said. 'He was born with . . .' He began again. 'He was born without a head.'

Anencephaly, she thought, with horror. Incompatible with life.

'When he was born he was just sort of . . .' He closed his eyes. 'Floppy. There was no life in him. No breath. He never cried. The doctors told us he couldn't live. And from then on Erica . . .'

So that was her name. His wife. Erica Randall.

He was still staring miserably out across the water, not at her. It was as though he had forgotten she was there. 'Erica changed,' he finished. 'She's had various diagnoses pinned on her.' He gave a cynical, bitter laugh. 'She's been diagnosed as bipolar, as having a psychopathic personality disorder. Some doctors insist she's schizophrenic, others that she's suffering from post-natal psychosis. I've heard it all and from one day to the next I never know what she's going to be like. Demonic, sometimes. Hateful. Frightening.' He looked across at her. 'I know what you're thinking, Martha. I know.' He looked tired, weary, older than his years. 'She . . . We came from Reading. She was . . .' His forehead was creased with anxiety and unhappiness. 'She was assaulting people.' That mirthless laugh again. 'Even me, which was embarrassing. She was breaking shop windows, shop-lifting, causing an affray, abusing people mentally and physically.' He gave a twisted smile. 'She seemed full of hatred. As you

143

can imagine, it didn't exactly do my career much good. In the end we decided it was best if we moved somewhere where we were not known and Erica had to succumb to treatment.'

Martha frowned. 'What sort of treatment?'

She knew. There was no treatment for a personality disorder. One just had to wait until they grew out of it. Or not.

He looked at her. 'They tried electroconvulsive therapy, which was awful and inappropriate anyway. Basically she's admitted if she fails to take major sedation. She's in hospital at the moment after smashing up the house. Again.' He looked at her then. 'I know what you're thinking . . .'

Oh, no, you don't.

'I could divorce her,' he said. 'Yes, I could. And how would that look? I dump a wife because she has psychiatric problems? Not good, but it'll all come out one day, Martha. She'll do something which will make it impossible for me to continue here. And then I'll become a fugitive again.'

A fugitive again.

She was surprised at how bleak this made her feel. Then she opened her eyes wide and spoke because the words had pricked her. 'A fugitive again,' she said. 'Like Charles?'

He started and she knew he was leaving his confession behind him.

She reached out and touched his hand. 'I am so sorry, Alex,' she said, 'about your home circumstances. I really am. I don't know what to say. I'd hoped . . .' She couldn't lie and say she'd hoped he was happily married but she couldn't leave the sentence unfinished.

'I'd hoped your personal life was less wretched,' she said finally and with honesty.

What possible solution could there be for this situation? She was puzzling this one out when he spoke.

'I wish she would die,' he said very softly, but she heard it as clearly as if he had shouted it from the rooftops. Clanged it like a church bell summoning the faithful to fervent Christian prayer. And it was a prayer.

I – wish – she – would – die.

But then what?

The thought frightened her.

Twenty

Randall detailed DS Paul Talith and DC Gethin Roberts to search Miss Dreyfuss's garden shed that 'Charles' had used as a doss house. He kept the name to himself, smiling when he thought of Martha's face, but then he recalled the way the conversation had turned and felt like dropping his face into his hands. His life was turning into a mess.

Oblivious to their SIO's anguish, Talith and Roberts had driven out to Pontesbury Hill and found Miss Dreyfuss in a pair of old trousers and gardening gloves looking at her flower beds ruefully.

'Truth is,' she said, looking up at them, despair clouding her face, 'I don't know how I'm going to manage this place now. He did an awful lot.'

Talith studied her features and read the despair. Despair and something else which, surprisingly, he identified as grief. She had liked their victim. He frowned. It was beginning to give colour to the man. The emotion of grief clothed bones with warm flesh, made blood flow in the veins, a pulse pump along the artery and blew air into the lungs of someone he had so far only thought of as an anonymous dead vagrant. Being in contact with someone who had known The Man and liked him was giving him a personality. He had been likeable. Talith was silent, still frowning. Someone mourned him. Then he looked across at Roberts, who was watching him, and toughened his attitude up. It didn't tell them who he was or where he had been or come from.

The shed was a bog standard wooden garden shed, made of roughly hewn wood and stained green. Talith had one like it at home, but a bit smaller. Once a year he and Diana cleared it out; the rest of the time it was an absolute tip, a chaos of lawnmowers and hedge clippers, rakes and hoes, sprays of weed killer, bags of compost, Weed 'n' Feed and other garden detritus. This was nothing like that. He and Roberts both stared. It was military: every tool carefully laid out, bottles lined up in order of size, bags of compost neatly stored, spades and other equipment hanging from hooks. In the corner there was a folded sun lounger on which were neatly folded blankets. So now they knew something else about their man. He was or had been methodical. Even Miss Dreyfuss seemed surprised at the orderliness. 'I rarely came in here,' she said quietly, peering past them from the doorway. 'It seemed – it was – his domain.'

Talith simply stared around the shed and breathed it in. It had the scent of a holiday caravan when you first joined it after a long, wet winter. Stuffy, needing airflow. He turned to Roberts. 'Know what this tidiness reminds me of?'

'Military?' Roberts ventured.

'No,' he said. 'Prison. You ever been in a cell, Roberts?'

The younger officer was affronted. ''Course I have, a time or two.'

147

Talith made a face. 'They're just like this, tidy in a small, contained space. Oppressively tidy, mate. We'd better get some pictures before the CS officers disturb it.'

And so Freddie Gascoigne, police photographer, was again summoned. He was having a busy day. And even he made a face when he eyed the orderliness of the shed.

'Bloody hell,' he said. 'Don't tell the wife. She'll have me scrubbing out our shed. This is tidier than our kitchen.'

The officers smiled at him. Bald and plump, under five foot six inches tall, Freddie was one of those people with a wonderful talent for making you smile. Maybe it was his face, stuck in an almost permanent grin, or maybe it was his constant merry quips that took the drama out of any situation.

While he was snapping away, Talith looked at Roberts with concern. 'What's the matter with you lately, Geth?'

Roberts shrugged. 'Nothing,' he said, eyes scanning the garden, his face pained and his features tight. He and Talith had always been good mates, both of them at the same point in their lives – about to take relationships further. Except . . . PC Gethin Roberts looked at his pal but didn't feel quite the same warmth towards him. He looked around him. Once he'd thought he and Flora might have a garden like this. Now he was not quite so sure. She'd recently gone all negative with him. They'd been going out for more than five years. She'd always been wide-eyed, innocent, easy to impress. But she'd changed. She didn't even want to . . . well. He met the sergeant's eyes, flushed and shrugged. 'Leave it,' he said gruffly, staring down at his big policeman's shoes. Somehow even they didn't see quite so great and impressive these days.

Freddie had finished his work. He was packing his equipment away. 'I'll get these sorted,' he said cheerfully, 'and email them across.' He held out his hand to shake. Gethin Roberts caught a flash of a wedding ring. *No wonder he was so bloody cheerful*, he thought, and felt sour inside.

He and Talith had a superficial look around the shed, moving bags and equipment, sprays of Pathclear, Weed 'n' Feed, trowels and garden forks. They took the sun lounger outside and shook out all the blankets. There appeared to be nothing of their man's personal effects except, stashed in a corner, they found one paltry possession: a grubby pink comb with a couple of teeth missing.

He bagged it up and put a label on it, his frown deepening.

There didn't seem to be much for the CS guys to find here. Best seal it up and have a word with the boss. No point wasting public money.

Randall had driven to the mortuary and was currently staring down at the dead man's face. Pale fish skin. Eyes forever shut. Mouth almost closed, chin held up by a bandage, but he could just see a wad of cotton wool that had been placed inside the mouth. 'To mop up any secretions,' Sullivan had explained.

Mercifully, the neck wound had a dressing over

it. Pointless, yes, but it at least concealed the ugly gash. 'No point in stitching it up,' Mark Sullivan had remarked cheerfully. 'It isn't going to heal.'

Randall shivered. He could feel the chill of the corpse-fridge emanating from Charles like the miasma from a medium's ghost, wrapping cold fingers around him.

'Who are you, Charlie, boy?' he asked.

Mark Sullivan, in blue scrubs, was standing behind. 'You'd have a bloody shock if he answered.'

Randall simply blew out a frustrated breath and the pathologist continued, 'No luck then with his ID?'

'Not so far.' Randall's eyes moved down over the white paper shroud to the label tied around the big toe of Charles's left foot, the ultimate indignity, and on it no name, simply:

Body 301
Cause of death: Homicide.
Date of Death: Thursday, 11 September
Post-mortem: Monday, 15 September
Sex: Male
ID: Unknown

It was not much of an epitaph and brought home the man's complete anonymity, which, according to the few witnesses who had known him alive, was just what he'd wanted. Why else would he keep his name a secret? More than ever, Randall wanted to find out who he was before they put him six feet under. He didn't want him in an unmarked grave.

Mark Sullivan put a friendly hand on his shoulder. 'I've got some news about the prosthesis, though not our man's identity. It was used in Switzerland in the nineties so I think skiing was responsible for the fracture.'

Randall nodded. 'We've had that confirmed by someone who knew him.'

'Someone knew him?'

'Yeah. He did some gardening for her. But here's the thing, Mark. She didn't know his name. He never told her.'

'Odd.' Then he grinned at Randall. 'So my guess was right. It was the result of a skiing accident. I only wish I'd put money on it.'

But Randall obviously wasn't himself. He simply grunted, failing to rise to the bait.

Mark Sullivan looked at him for a moment before he continued, 'They use a different prosthesis nowadays, so we can be fairly sure of the period of the injury.'

Randall turned around. 'Do they keep records?'

'Yes, but they don't seem to be able access them just at the moment, so we're no further forward.'

Randall was irritated. 'Don't they keep a database?'

'Yes – somewhere – but there are a lot to get through. There are a lot of skiing accidents, Alex. Their records are not on a computer database so it's a matter of going through them by hand.'

He gave Randall a swift glance. *Definitely not himself.*

As though to underline that, Randall looked down at Charles and felt a sudden burst of

151

frustration. 'Who are you really?' Then, 'Who *were* you? *What* were you? Why has it been so important to keep your identity a secret?'

The pathologist gave a chuckle. 'He's not going to tell you, Alex. You're going to have to find out through good detective work. And where does the "Charlie" come from?'

Randall pushed the shelf back into the mortuary fridge. 'Martha,' he said. 'She calls him Charlie.'

Mark Sullivan was curious. 'Why?' He slammed the door shut.

'Well, Charlie Chaplin, the tramp, you know?' Randall followed the pathologist back into his office and they sat and had a companionable coffee together.

Mark Sullivan started asking questions. 'You know nothing more about him, Alex?'

'Well – a little. Not very much,' he admitted. 'The nuns knew him but it doesn't seem they ever really engaged him in conversation, although they say that Charles was a Catholic. I wonder whether he ever made a confession.'

'Are they and the woman he gardened for the only ones who knew him?'

'No. The girls at McDonald's gave him chips sometimes. A lorry driver gave him a lift out to Moreton Corbet. It seems to have been pure chance that he ended up there. The woman he did some gardening for was an ex-headmistress and he dossed sometimes in her shed. Oddly enough, she described him as cultured.' He smiled to himself. 'That's why I think "Charlie" is a little irreverent. "Charles" seems a bit more dignified.'

'I see. Any other clues?'

Randall shook his head and sat back in his chair. 'What I want, as well as his name, is his backstory. I want to know why this man, who appeared to know about gardening and hummed opera and went skiing, became a vagrant in the first place. And even more than that I want to know who cut his bloody throat.' He put his coffee cup back on Mark Sullivan's desk and rose. 'I ought to be getting back,' he said. 'I won't find my answers here.'

'You might,' Sullivan rejoined, seeing him to the door. 'You never know.'

'We'll see.'

Twenty-One

The follow-up visit to McDonald's wasn't a great deal of help. One girl, Lisa, appeared to remember him but had obviously classed him generically as 'one of the tramps' and not paid particular attention to him.

PC Delia Shaw decided to visit the charity shops to see if anyone could identify the coat and trousers The Man had been wearing. This was the fourth one she'd visited that morning but really she should have started here. The shop, on Wyle Cop's steep incline, gave the clue. It was called *Missing*, and its windows sported photographs of people with the text, *Lost to their families*. Underneath the pictures and text was another objective. *Help us to reunite them.*

She pushed open the door. In her heart of hearts she was dubious that this line of enquiry would bear fruit. The Man might have been given it by anyone or even stolen it from one of the clothes depositaries which had appeared at the recycling plant, in town car parks and outside supermarkets. Even if he had acquired it from a charity shop, she didn't think the assistants would necessarily remember him. There was a huge turnover of part-time helpers in these shops. Even if the assistant did remember him, chances were that she wouldn't be able to add anything to their paltry store of facts about the dead man. So as she

154

approached the sales desk she was not optimistic, until she showed the assistant a picture of the coat and watched her eyes light up in recognition. Shaw was due some luck and she felt hopeful. Then reality stepped in. The Man, whom DI Randall appeared to now call 'Charles' for some God-knew-what reason, had made a deliberate attempt to keep his identity a tight secret. He'd never told anybody his name or any of his personal details. Having succeeded in keeping his secret for a number of years, he was hardly likely to have blabbed it all out to the girl behind the counter in a charity shop. Even if the shop was called *Missing*.

It was hard to say exactly how old Phoebe Walker was. Perhaps in her late thirties, but possibly younger. She could have been in her forties or even her fifties – a big woman who wore big boots and a full-skirted homespun dress, and tied her hair back in a thick brown ponytail with an elastic band.

PC Shaw held up her ID and said her bit. 'We're investigating the death of a vagrant whose body was found in this coat. We're wondering whether it came from a charity shop . . .' She looked around vaguely. 'Perhaps yours or one of the others.' So far, although the assistants in every shop had displayed prurient curiosity, no one had given her any information. And she was losing heart.

Phoebe Walker examined the coat slowly and very carefully, her mouth pursed and her hands touching the rough tweed. 'I gave it to him,' she said tentatively, as though she expected a scolding for her actions. 'I didn't think Mr Knebworth would mind. The man looked cold and, after all, our charity's aimed at the homeless and people with no fixed abode.'

PC Shaw took a leap into the dark. 'Did you give him a pair of trousers too?'

The girl nodded. 'They belonged to Mr Knebworth,' she said and repeated, 'I didn't think he'd mind.'

Twenty-Two

PCs Sean Dart and Gary Coleman were down amongst the homeless in Silks Meadow, a small field in Frankwell near the new council offices. Most of them had erected some sort of home – a sheet of plastic, a bin liner over a sleeping bag; a few had a huddle of blankets, while others simply sat, head in hands. It was eight p.m.; dusk gave the field an air of surrealism, of faded lives, of hopelessness, squalor and despair. The weather was cool but not cold and yet there was a depressingly damp chill that seemed to emanate not only from the nearby river and the ground but from the people themselves. There was a strange feeling of absence, of a void, a vacuum of life which both PCs found disturbing.

Walking through the damp field, they had a feeling they had entered the land of the undead. That they were walking through war-wounded men after one of the great slaughtering battles: the battle of Shrewsbury, the Somme, Dunkirk. It was as if life and hope had been sucked out of them by events. Some of them met them with red eyes, but most looked away. A vague scent of marijuana clung to the air. Many were smoking, roll ups mainly; a few swigged from bottles. The background sound was a soft mumbling but there was no conversation. No words. They mumbled to themselves and spoke inside themselves, not to each other. There was no communication. Most patently didn't want to engage with the two officers either.

So Coleman and Dart strode through the field, taking care not to step on the few who were already unconscious, stretched out face up as though sunbathing on a beach. Even though the two officers were in uniform, wearing Day-Glo vests as well as a girdle of equipment, which clanked as they walked, many seemed not to notice them, aiming their gazes beyond them as though the two policemen were invisible or perhaps not in their world.

Perhaps they inhabited an alternative universe. Even though one of their loose family had died a violent death, no one seemed to be interested in the intruders or want to engage with them. They addressed a few but there was only negation, a shaking of heads followed by a drop of the face and a shrug. No one told them anything. PCs Coleman and Dart looked at each other, incredulous. They simply couldn't believe it. By their calculation The Man had been hanging around Shrewsbury for around five years. The nuns' statements combined with the vague statements from the girls at McDonald's suggested this, even though he had only been helping Genevieve Dreyfuss out for three years. He had certainly been one of their number for a while, yet amongst his fellow vagrants no one seemed to want to find out who had killed him.

Except . . . He was young – looked no older than fourteen, with darting blue eyes and a mop of sandy hair, sitting on the grass propped up

158

against a litter bin. Unlike the others, he didn't smell unwashed, but of deodorant. His clothes, ripped jeans and a hoodie, were relatively clean and his eyes held a spark of something. Life? He eyed the two officers uncertainly then nodded. They waited for him to say the first word.

'You 'ere about him? The one what got . . .' He drew his finger deliberately and slowly across his throat.

They nodded, resisting the temptation to play stupid, ask him about whom or to alternatively play the policeman and question him about his age, his name, his origins.

They simply prompted, 'Did you know him?'

As expected, this provoked a shifty gaze out across the river where Darwin's sculpture rose like a dinosaur's curved spine. 'Sort of.'

More or less the answer they'd been anticipating.

Gary Coleman hunkered down beside him. 'What did you know about him?'

The blue eyes turned shifty.

Coleman tried again, appealing for information. 'We haven't even been able to find out his name,' he said.

The boy's eyes were bright. 'He used to talk in his sleep, you know. I heard him.'

Coleman struggled to appear nonchalant. 'Did he say anything that might help us find his killer?'

'I don't know, do I?'

Inside, Coleman almost groaned. He had to put this on – this bravado. 'What did he say?'

The boy looked at him, frowning, as though disturbed by his story. 'Stuff like he'd scream

and say *"not you"* and then he'd say *"splash".*
And then, *"Take the money. Have it. Have it all."*
Then, *"Knock, knock, knock, I must finish these
shoes."* He mimicked a soft, wild voice, his accent
and words different from his native tongue. He
was a good mimic.

'And then . . .' He hesitated, suddenly realizing
this had a value. The sparkle in his eyes was now
pure greed. Was there anything in this for him?

Dart fingered a twenty-pound note. It'd go on
smack or hash, spliffs or fags and cider, the
banquet of the vagrant, but hey . . . He handed
it to him.

The boy took it, scanned it as though examining
it for fraud. Cheeky bugger, Coleman thought.
Then the boy half closed his eyes and sniffed as
though already breathing in a joint.

They wouldn't get much more out of him, was
Coleman's next thought. He was wrong.

Their boy spoke again. *"'One hundred and five,
north tower,'"* he said, adding his own interpreta-
tion. 'I reckon the poor guy'd been in prison for
some time.'

But Coleman and Dart knew he hadn't. They'd
have had his fingerprints if he had, but no need
to say this to the lad. 'Did he ever say a name?'

'Yeah. Lucy. He cried it a couple of times but
when he woke up and I asked him who Lucy
was he looked blank.'

The two officers exchanged puzzled glances.

'Anything more?' PC Sean Dart asked, but the
boy shook his head.

'Nah,' he said. 'Nuffin.'

They took his details and advised him to use

160

the shelter as a base for applying for work. This earned them a glance that would wither a flower. Before they left, Dart bent over and spoke softly in the boy's ear. 'Is there anyone looking for you?'

Unexpectedly, the boy's eyes filled with tears as he shook his head. 'No,' he said.

'You're sure there's no one out there wondering where you are who would want to know you're safe and well?'

Again the boy shook his head, and they left. They hadn't got much but it was something more to add to their paltry little stack of knowledge.

'Did you get it all down?'

Sean Dart nodded. 'Every word,' he said.

Friday, 19 September, 9 a.m.

It had been in desperation that Randall had released pictures of the child's shoe and also of the war medals, but it had brought in a shower of phone calls all telling them the same thing – details they already knew about the various campaigns for which the medals were awarded. Though their callers were trying to be helpful, not one of them was able to shed any light on the identity of Charles and Randall felt even more frustrated. They'd been deflecting phone calls from ex-servicemen for hours. Maybe releasing pictures of the medals hadn't been such a great idea after all.

He listened with interest to Coleman and Dart's account of their walk amongst the homeless but could not make any sense of it. His eyes narrowed

161

at the description of Miss Dreyfuss's garden shed but, like Roberts and Talith, he agreed that there wasn't much point in stripping the place bare. It sounded as though they had done a pretty good job. They gave him the comb almost apologetically and assured him there was nothing more to find.

'OK,' he said. 'For now we'll seal up the shed. If we need to we may get the crime scene investigators to run through it but . . .' He made his decision. 'For now we'll wait.'

Randall was silent for a moment, his gaze wandering around the room. Then he spoke abruptly. 'I thought I'd go back out to Moreton Corbet this afternoon. I want to speak to Mr Sharp. Come with me, PC Dart.'

Sean looked startled at this but nodded. He felt a little apprehensive at the invitation. Was it a chance for DI Randall to make some negative observation? He didn't want to move on. He'd found a niche here. OK, he wasn't exactly welcome yet but he thought he could carve a life out here and leave the past behind him. He clung on to his mantra. After the nightmare comes the dream. And he knew who he was dreaming about.

Publishing the picture of the shoes had attracted other attention. Someone from the museum at Blists Hill had rung, a brisk lady with a slight speech impediment when she pronounced her 'r's, and explained to Randall that they had a pair of shoes just like that in one of their Victorian cottages. She then went into great detail to tell him they were made of calf leather and the soles wood hob nailed. 'The nails,' she said pompously, 'were, of course, handmade.' But when Randall asked if a pair of their shoes was missing she became flustered. 'No,' she said. 'I looked. They're still there.'

Randall remained polite, asked her if she knew of any other museums in the area that might have similar exhibits, and when she said no, she didn't think so, he thanked her and put the phone down. So what had been the bloody use of that? he wondered. It had simply been an education, though they'd already gleaned as much from the lady at Shrewsbury Museum.

And he was interested in shoes? Actually, no. What he was interested in was finding out who the bloody man was and who had slit his throat.

And why had the crime scene yielded so little pertinent evidence? As an area visited by numbers of the general public there was plenty of evidence but nothing specific to either their victim or his killer. It was all very frustrating.

PC Delia Shaw gave her report of her encounter at *Missing*.

She'd described Phoebe Walker so Randall could picture her. Homespun, kind-hearted. One of the good people.

'She said he came into the shop months ago during the winter. He'd said he was cold.

It was a horrible day.' She smiled and quoted. '"A rotten, icy wind blowing right up the Cop. Freezing. I felt so sorry for him."' Shaw paused. 'She said he was proud. He had a ten-pound note and offered it to her for the coat. And, unbelievably, she said that his next words had been, "It'll help the homeless." She couldn't believe it and said, '"He was bloody homeless himself."'

'She said she couldn't have taken his money and told him the coat was a gift from Mr Knebworth himself, that he wouldn't mind her giving it to him, that that was the point of the shop – to help people like him.'

Shaw was silent. The worm of an idea was wriggling inside her brain.

'She told him to go and buy himself some hot soup and keep warm.' She looked around the room. 'And then she said she knew they were supposed to make as much money from their gifts as they could but a life is a life – one life could not be more precious than another.'

Her colleagues were silent, listening to the PC's words.

'She was confused by something. He said, "Thank you, Lucy."'

Randall's ears pricked up, recalling the words of the vagrant as reported by Coleman and Dart. 'She looked quite bewildered, sir, and said, "My name's Phoebe. And he didn't know that anyway. I didn't tell him. He didn't know my name. So why did he call me Lucy? I didn't understand it then and I don't understand it now."'

Randall spoke. 'Did she say anything more about him?'

'No – just what we've already heard: that he was accentless, that he seemed a nice man. Same sort of stuff.'

'Wait a minute,' Randall said. 'When she said that the coat had been a gift from Mr Knebworth himself, did she mean through the charity or that it had actually belonged to Mr Knebworth?'

Sean Dart started. The name Knebworth meant something to him – that connection with the wife of a man who had caused mayhem in a drink driving incident and subsequently vanished.

'I'm sorry,' Delia Shaw was saying. 'I'm not absolutely sure. I suppose she could have meant either. I got the impression that the coat and trousers had actually belonged to Mr Knebworth, but I can check.'

She pressed on: 'I did ask her whether Mr Knebworth had much to do with the homeless and she said, yes, he did loads. He and his wife served in the soup kitchen, sometimes spent a night with them. She said they helped in the shop sometimes and that the staff all thought they were wonderful.'

Mr and Mrs Wonderful, Randall thought. Time he spoke to them.

'Was there anything else?'

'He asked for a pen and she lent him one. She said, "What's a pen, after all?"'

It was a question Delia Shaw asked herself all the way back to the nick. As far as she remembered their man had not had a pen amongst his personal possessions. Or anything to write on.

The quote swam into her head about the pen being mightier than the sword. Only it hadn't been, had it? She smiled to herself. Shaw dismissed the quote as being fanciful. His throat hadn't been cut with a bloody pen. It had been cut with something much more predictable – a kitchen knife.

Twenty-Three

Friday, 19 September, 5 p.m.

Martha had called on a friend of hers. Miranda Mountford had been her buddy ever since she and Martin had moved to Shrewsbury almost twenty years ago, she heavily pregnant with twins, little suspecting that her husband possibly already had growing inside him the tumour that would kill him two years later. Miranda had supported her through that terrible time just as Martha had supported her through an awful period in her life – the violent separation from her husband. And so the friendship had been cemented.

She met her in town, on an afternoon that had turned suddenly stormy, blowing many people's umbrellas inside out. Martha hated umbrellas almost as much as she hated any waterproof head-gear, hoods or mackintosh hats, finding them restrictive. She liked her hair to blow free – even in rainstorms, a habit that earned her the wrath of Vernon Grubb, her beefy hairdresser. She still allowed her hair to blow free in wind and rain, knowing he would 'tut, tut' when next she visited him. But the result of her prejudice was that when she reached the coffee shop her hair was streaming cold rivulets down her neck.

Miranda had worked in Public Health and her

167

husband, Steven, had grown increasingly hostile and pathological toward his wife, jealous of her success in her own field of work. The marriage had finally ended in an acrimonious divorce and a necessary court order against him, and the last Martha had heard he was in South Africa – a source of relief to her friend. Since then her life had moved on and she had recently elected to work part-time and help in a charity: *Missing*. She would be killing two birds with one stone, meeting up with a friend and maybe finding out more about the charity.

Miranda was there before her, already sitting with a mug of coffee, reading one of the newspapers which were to hand. She had a blonde bob in the style she'd worn for at least twenty years, and two children, both now grown up: Mark, a banker in New York, and Prue, who ran a bar/restaurant in Madeira. Most of her holidays were spent visiting one or the other and Martha planned to join her on one of her trips. Either destination would suit her. Looking delighted, Miranda stood up when Martha arrived and kissed her on the cheek. 'Well, hello, stranger,' she said, grinning broadly. 'How are you? You look wonderful, but . . .'

Martha held up her hand. 'I know what you're going to say. You haven't seen me for ages. I've been busy.'

Miranda's eyes sparkled. 'Working alongside Detective Inspector Alex Randall?'

'And others,' Martha said firmly.

Miranda sat down again, eyeing her over the rim of her coffee mug. 'But none of your other work colleagues make you go quite as red in the face, darling,' she said.

Martha ignored the comment, which did not escape her friend's attention. She gave her a sharp look and continued, 'Now let me guess,' finger on chin. 'You want to pump me about a certain homeless man who has been violently dispatched?'

Martha nodded. 'Yes. You saw the pictures in the paper, Miranda?'

'Oh, yes. Shocking. It's horrible to see someone you've known feature on the front page of the paper like that. Poor man.'

'You knew him?' Martha was astonished.

Miranda didn't answer straight away but thought for a moment then shook her head. 'No,' she said. 'I couldn't say I knew him but I was an acquaintance. He was one of the people I dealt with.'

'Have you told the police that?'

'Of course I have, but all they wanted to know were facts. You, Martha, will be asking me something quite different. *You* will want my *impression* of him. *They* asked straight questions. Did I know his name? Did I know where he came from? Did I know if he had any friends, relatives? It was all questions. I didn't *know* anything.'

'What was he like?'

'Polite, quiet. Reticent.'

'Why? Why would he be reticent?'

'I can only give you my impression, Martha. I thought that he had perhaps decided to turn his back on society or at least on someone or something. He was well spoken but refused to engage with any of us. He would answer questions but not volunteer information. And before you ask,' she said as Martha opened her mouth to speak, 'he never gave me his name. He said once, when I asked him, that it would be useless him giving me his name.'

'Why?'

'I asked him and he just smiled and said, "Believe me, Mrs Mountford, my name will not be helpful to you. My name does not exist anymore. Not in the land of the living."'

'"Not in the land of the living"?' Martha frowned. 'Was he a drunk?'

'He did drink but I never saw him drunk or heard him incoherent.'

'Schizophrenic?'

'No.'

'Did he take drugs?'

'No.'

'So what . . .?'

Miranda simply touched her friend's hand. 'He said he did not exist anymore, that he was a non-person.'

'Well, I . . .' For once, Martha Gunn, coroner, was flummoxed, at a loss for words.

'There was one thing more,' her friend added. 'As you know, the men – they are mostly men – go to the shelter and sometimes sit at a table. Your gentleman would sit alone.'

Knowing what she did, Martha was not surprised to hear this, but her friend's next words did surprise her.

'He'd spend the time scribbling in an exercise book.'

'What?'

Miranda looked smug. 'So it hasn't been found amongst his belongings?'

'Not as far as I know.'

'Well then,' her friend said, smiles creasing her face, 'it gives you the perfect excuse to ring Alex.'

Twenty-Four

Friday, 19 September, 6 p.m.

Randall had taken Sean Dart with him. He wanted to speak to Rufus Sharp, gentleman farmer, for himself and see his face when he asked his question.

He also wanted to speak again to the other inhabitants of Moreton Corbet: John Hyde, finder of the body, who lived in another farmworker's cottage in the village, and Wilfred Hook. He wanted to meet them all for himself, including Wilfred's Labrador, Imogen. Like PC Gary Coleman, Randall had a weakness for Golden Labradors. Lovely dogs. Dart had been right when he'd shot that nervous, worried glance at him when he had issued the instruction that he accompany him on this visit. He did want to keep PC Dart close to him. He wanted to observe his new recruit's behaviour. Get a handle on the man. The truth was a vacancy would be coming up soon for a detective constable and he wanted to decide whether Dart was suitable material. He had done well so far, but before he let him into the ranks he wanted to be sure.

He began with the person he anticipated would give him the most trouble – Rufus Sharp of Moreton Corbet Farm, who lived opposite the castle.

He had the idea that Sharp would object strongly to having had a vagrant hanging around the village at all, let alone one who was inconsiderate enough to have his throat cut at an historic site right opposite his own front door. Randall knew from experience that some landowners could be arrogant, holding the belief that because they owned land they had a right to privacy over and above their neighbours. They could be bully boys. But cutting a tramp's throat? He didn't really think so. Then again, had he seen their man descend from the lorry delivering the animal feed on that September evening?

There was only one way to make this judgement – see for himself. He outlined his thoughts to PC Sean Dart and waited for him to make some comment. None came. Randall eyed him curiously. This was a man who kept his cards very, very close to his chest. So close it was hard to know what was going on in his mind. He knew Dart had transferred to Shrewsbury due to some problem. He knew it must have been bad. He didn't really know anything more but he wondered about him – as did the others in the station. But PC Dart was not telling.

He knocked on Sharp's stout front door and it was pulled open by a very attractive slim blonde lady in jodhpurs. Randall was taken aback. She looked very young. 'Mrs Sharp?'

'Yes.' She had a lovely voice, light and clean as a lemon, and her smile initially appeared equally refreshing.

Randall displayed his card and explained. He admired her face. Perfect and beautiful, and she was able to convey no emotion but regarded him with a face that was a blank canvas. Randall looked closer. A man had been cruelly killed practically on her doorstep and she showed no emotion? No fear or apprehension or even curiosity. Weird. The smile seemed pasted on to her face. He glanced at PC Dart, whose dark eyes also registered nothing.

So Randall addressed Mrs Sharp with a touch of irony. 'I hope you're not too threatened by these events?'

'Well, we've never had such a police presence,' she said coolly. 'If anything I feel safer with them around.' She gave him a confident smile displaying spectacularly white and even teeth which, oddly enough, made Randall revise his opinion of her. He wasn't sure he liked her. She was too chilly. Too cool and too distant. Too manufactured perfect. She felt synthetic.

'Have you ever seen a hobo, a tramp, a vagrant hanging around here?'

'Never,' she said firmly. 'Your officers have already asked us that on numerous occasions.'

'Oh.' There was no disputing the boredom with which she had said this.

He'd had enough of her. 'Is your husband in?'

'Somewhere,' she said airily, and Randall decided he really didn't like her at all. The old world of surfs and landowners, peasants and gentry had always rankled with him, though he wouldn't have called himself overly sensitive as to the question of class. But this beautiful woman with her porcelain skin and fragrant air was frankly irritating. 'Then would you please go and get him?'

Visibly annoyed that her charm didn't appear to be working, she tightened her lips and gave him a sulky look, pushed the door ajar and disappeared, almost rudely closing it behind her. Moments later they heard her voice whining. Randall couldn't resist smirking at PC Dart, who shot him a look back. A minute stretched into two then three, and finally the door was tugged open.

Sharp's scowl was thunderous. 'Now what?'

In a clipped voice, equally tight-lipped, Randall explained who he was.

It didn't do much to improve Sharp's manners. 'Your traffic and the general increase of people is causing a devil of a fuss here. We can hardly get the tractors up the lane. Do you know when you'll be gone?'

'We're investigating a murder,' Randall said angrily. 'We'll be going when we're ready.'

Sharp contented himself with a heavy sigh.

'This isn't a social call,' Randall continued, his hostility compounding by the minute. 'I'm not here to apologize but to see whether you have anything to add to your statement, whether you've remembered something that might help us . . .' his eyes flickered, '. . . to hone in on the man who slit this poor fellow's throat.' He paused, adding maliciously, hoping Sharp's wife was listening in from behind the door, 'Practically on your doorstep, Mr Sharp.'

Sharp looked away, veiling his true emotion. But his voice, when he spoke, was more conciliatory. 'I'm sorry,' he said. 'Life has just been a little more difficult lately.'

'Is there anything you can think of that might help us to find out who did this horrible thing?'

Sharp shook his head.

Randall eyed him speculatively. 'The night before we found the man's body,' he began, 'Thursday, September the eleventh, you had a delivery of animal feed late in the afternoon.'

Sharp looked bemused. 'And?'

'The lorry driver, Mr Nelson Futura, had picked up our man from just outside the Shrewsbury bypass.'

Sharp looked wary now.

'He dropped him off here. Did you see him?'

Sharp frowned. 'I don't remember,' he said.

'Think,' Randall prompted.

'I'm not sure.'

'Did you see him descend from the lorry's cab?'

Sharp blew out a heavy, annoyed sigh. 'If I did, it didn't register,' he said. 'As I say, I've had a lot on my plate recently. I've been quite distracted.'

Randall waited a minute but nothing more was forthcoming and they left. He couldn't be certain whether Sharp had seen their man descend from the lorry or not. And if he had seen him, whether there would be any reason for denying the fact.

He glanced at Sean Dart but again PC Dart offered no comment and Alex Randall didn't either except to say, 'Well, shall we try the cottage?'

As they walked up the drive of Moreton Corbet Cottage Imogen bounded towards them, tongue hanging out, tail wagging as though electrified.

Randall bent down and stroked the coarse

176

golden coat. He wasn't a great dog lover but somehow Golden Labradors seemed to ease themselves right into his heart. Imogen looked up at him, her brown eyes beseeching and, unconsciously mirroring Coleman's response, Randall felt his heart melt. If he ever had a dog again she would be like this one. His heart was still melting as he scratched behind her ears and addressed his first question to the dog. 'Did you see anything, Imogen?' he asked her, and she wagged her tail even harder.

Wilfred was working in the garden in spite of the drizzle of rain which, in the last ten minutes, had dropped like a grey chiffon curtain across the scene, endowing it with an air of mystery so the cottage garden no longer looked like the scene of child's picnic but someplace strange and slightly ghost-like. Hook held up a plastic flower pot to explain what he was doing. 'Slugs,' he said. 'Best to get them in the rain. Don't like using pellets,' he further explained. 'Poisons the thrushes, you know.'

Randall nodded his appreciation of the sight of the pot oozing with slimy wet bodies.

'Did you ever see a vagrant around here, Mr Hook?'

'I saw someone who looked like a vagrant in the church one day, about a month ago,' he said. 'I was surprised. Though it was a warm day he was wearing a huge coat. He shuffled out without responding to my greeting. I think it might have been your man and I told one of the officers. But I'm sorry . . .' And he really did look sorry, 'I have nothing further to add. I wish I did. I couldn't even describe him.' Then he changed tack. 'I'm not exactly easy with this situation, you know, living so near a crime scene.'

And you expect me to do exactly what? Move it?

'It is difficult,' Randall responded with the empathetic politically correct phrase. 'We'll be gone as soon as we can and people will forget.'

Wilfred shook his head. 'Oh, no, they won't. People don't forget. This place will always be remembered for this happening. Everyone who comes here in future will come with a ghoulish expectation and look for bloodstains in the dining chamber or the tower. They'll take selfies slumped in the corner pretending to be your unknown corpse and try to scrape up what they think are bloodstains on the steps. Oh, no . . .' His eyes wandered across to the castle. 'This place'll be forever tainted.'

Randall didn't bother denying this. It was probably true.

And again, Wilfred Hook changed direction. 'I expect my cottage will drop in price after this business.' Then he added as an afterthought, as though he realized his comments would have sounded heartless, 'The poor man.'

'Quite.' Randall frowned. 'Did you see anything the night of the murder, Mr Hook?'

'No.' Then denial came swift and vehement. 'It was such a nasty night,' he said, then repeated, 'such a nasty night. I had the curtains drawn, music on. Imogen was slumped by the fire. Though . . .' Something had struck him. 'She did start barking around eightish.' His eyes now

178

looked troubled. 'Do you think that was when . . .?'

Randall could tell he didn't want to finish the sentence. 'It's possible,' he said. 'It's certainly within the time frame.'

'Oh . . .' Hook looked even more troubled and Randall could guess what he was thinking.

'If it's any consolation, Mr Hook, I don't think you could have prevented our man's murder.'

'No.'

Something struck the detective. 'Is there a Mrs Hook?'

Wilfred drew in a deep breath and the dog rubbed her head against his shin. 'Somewhere,' he said resignedly. 'She left two years ago now. Went to live with her sister.' He looked at Randall with a confused look. 'I don't really know why,' he said. Then, stooping to rub the dog's head, added, with a hint of bravado, 'There's just the two of us now. We're quite happy, aren't we, Imo?'

The dog gave a contented yap.

'I've no understanding of women,' was Hook's final comment, and Randall heartily agreed.

'OK,' he said. 'Thank you.'

They left.

There was only John Hyde left, custodian of the castle. He too had nothing to add to the statement he had initially given to Gethin Roberts, though he was bending over backwards to try and help them, almost going so far as to improvise his evidence. Both Dart and Randall sensed that Hyde was actually enjoying the increased attention. Randall had suggested that the PC conduct the interview. It would give him a chance to observe him in action.

'Good gracious,' Hyde said, puffing his chest out in response to Dart's first question. 'The TV reporter asked me to relate the turn of events. Such a thing . . .' He flushed. 'I've never been on the TV before. Felt quite embarrassed.'

Sean Dart watched him from beneath lowered lids. 'Hope you didn't say anything . . .' He smiled, 'that you may later rely on in evidence.'

Hyde blew out his cheeks and went red. 'Of course not. Hah.' And then, 'That was a joke, I take it. I mean, I'm not really under suspicion, am I?'

Dart used typical policeman speak. 'Not at this moment in time, sir.' Then he took pity on the man. 'It must have been quite a shock, finding him.'

Hyde looked at him gratefully. 'I'm glad you understand, Constable. I'm going to find it very hard to open up shop for English Heritage in future.' He tried to laugh it off with an uncomfortable and false sounding, 'Hah, hah.'

'Do you feel uneasy living so near the crime scene?'

Hyde looked almost ashamed. 'I know it's silly,' he said, then, hiding behind a cliché, 'but lightning doesn't strike twice in the same place, does it?' His question tagged on the end made him sound a man very uneasy with recent events.

'Right,' PC Dart said, neither agreeing nor disagreeing. 'I don't suppose you've remembered anything else about that morning – or even the evening before?'

'I've tried to wrack my brains,' Hyde said. 'I'd love to help you. I really would. The only thing I want to do now is to open the gates again and invite people to come back and look at this wonderful place. I hate it deserted and empty, no one but the media and the police. It doesn't feel right.' His last add-on sounded petulant. 'The weather was good at the weekend but the only people here were the police. I felt sad, deserting the old lady.'

Sean Dart smiled. 'Is that how you think of her?'

'Truth is it is, rather. I have an affinity for the old thing.' He smiled. 'Bit of a wreck just like me. We've both seen better days.'

'But you haven't remembered anything else that might help us, some small detail?' Dart urged hopefully.

'Unfortunately, no. I've sat in my chair and thought really hard about it. I can't remember anything except what I've already told you boys. It was an ordinary morning. Wet, of course, after the rain. I unlocked the gate and inspected the site.'

'What made you look into the cellar?' Dart persisted. 'Do you normally check it out? Had you had tramps sleeping in there before?'

'Not to my knowledge. I mean, usually there's some rubbish dumped there and I have known people to use the place as a urinal. I generally take a bucket of disinfected water down there every now and then and swish it out, you know.'

Dart nodded and pushed forward with his question. 'So what made you go into the cellar?'

'I saw a splash of blood.'

Which had been on the third step down. Dart pondered the question. *Had there been something else?*

'And at what point did you see the man?'

'We-ell . . .' The question seemed to put him in some difficulty. 'I went down the steps.' He was thinking hard about this one – too hard, in Dart's opinion. His story should come more naturally.

Hyde continued, 'I saw something huddled in the corner. I thought he was asleep. I didn't see the wound. It didn't occur to me he was dead.' Even now, a week later, he still looked shocked. Sean Dart observed him carefully. And was convinced the guy was kosher. Honest.

During the drive back, Randall asked Dart if they had learned anything from the trip out to Moreton Corbet.

'We've probably narrowed down the time of death, sir. Sometime after Mr Futura dropped him off at five and Imogen hearing something at eight.'

Randall turned to look at him. 'We might have a narrower corridor of time of death, Sean,' he said, 'but it doesn't advance us much, does it?'

'It might, sir.'

And Randall smiled. Maybe Dart would make a good detective after all.

For himself, he was glad to have met the neighbours but it hadn't brought him any nearer to unlocking the case. And also, PC Dart, he felt, was deliberately keeping his true self carefully hidden.

Twenty-Five

Monday, 22 September, 8.30 a.m.

Randal picked PC Shaw up at the station at half past eight. She'd obviously dressed for the occasion in a neatly pressed uniform and looked lively. They'd tracked Graham Knebworth down to a modern gated house in High Ercol, a small village east of Shrewsbury. The place was immaculate, if a little soulless, the houses large, square, uncompromising and worth well over a million, with electric gates, lawns and manicured drives. Randall wondered just how Knebworth had made his money and why he had subsequently decided to found a charity for the homeless and disaffected.

Giving PC Shaw an encouraging grin, he knocked on the door. They'd already informed him that they would be calling and he had seemed perfectly happy with this arrangement.

Randall wasn't sure what he'd expected. His experience of philanthropists was limited but the man who pulled the door open certainly was nothing like he had anticipated.

Knebworth looked about sixty, an ageing rocker in tight, skinny jeans. He had a shock of white hair and his eyes were blue and as sharp and clear as icebergs. He spoke first. 'You must be Detective Inspector Randall,' he said with a

183

hearty handshake. 'And . . .?' He grinned at PC Shaw, who blushed and supplied her name.

Knebworth grinned at the policewoman. 'Yes, of course, PC Shaw,' he said. 'Come in. Come in.'

The warmth of the welcome was not what either of them had expected. They looked at each with vague confusion. Randall gave the slightest of shrugs and they followed Knebworth into a long hall with pale walls and a beige carpet. Watercolours lined the walls.

He led them into a long, lovely room, which seemed bathed in sunshine in spite of the cool day. A grand piano stood at one end in front of huge French windows which overlooked a lake and grounds and on into the distance.

Knebworth stood in front of it, staring out, obviously deriving great pleasure from the view. He invited them to share it. 'Lovely, isn't it?'

'Yes.' It was out before Shaw could stop it.

'Now, then.' Knebworth's hand went out, indicating they should sit, and he did the same. 'I can guess what all this is about. The poor old guy who got himself killed out at Moreton Corbet.'

'Correct,' Alex Randall said, reflecting that the 'poor old guy' had been about fifteen years younger than Knebworth.

'So . . .' He looked at both of them. 'How do you think I can help you?'

'We're having trouble,' Randall began awkwardly, 'finding out who he is.'

Knebworth didn't look surprised but offered no comment. His eyes, though, were wary.

'We don't . . .' Randall continued even more awkwardly, 'even know his name.'

'I see.'

'So we wondered if you might be able to help us.'

Knebworth's eyes narrowed and his expression was guarded.

He sat back in his chair and waited. PC Shaw gave Randall a swift, worried look.

But his returning glance was placid. He could wait.

Finally Knebworth gave a deep sigh. 'I can't tell you much,' he said. 'I knew him but nothing personal about him. We talked, you know, once or twice. He knew some of the places I'd been to.'

Randall interrupted. 'Do you know anything about his background?'

Knebworth shook his head. 'Close as the grave, he was, and what he didn't want people to know they never would.'

'Do you know his real name?'

Knebworth shook his head. 'Nah,' he said. Then he grinned at them and changed the subject. 'I expect you're wondering how I made all this,' he said.

Randall could do nothing but nod while PC Shaw looked at the carpet. It was a thick pile close enough to white. Pure wool, at a guess.

Knebworth laughed. 'Simple,' he said, speaking quickly. 'I left home as a teenager. Spent a few years on the streets of London. I know what it's like to be homeless, rootless. When I was sheltering under a bridge one night, freezing cold and feeling like I could eat the bloody thing, I made up a song about it. Nothing ventured, I thought, so next morning I spruced myself up and made my way to a house where I knew one of the members of the most famous band in the world lived. And I sang this song to him. He liked it. They recorded it but I kept all the copyright. Next thing I know they're using it in a film. And then some. And now . . .' he waved his hand around him, 'I live here. And who do I help?' Suddenly he leaned forward, hands at an awkward angle on his knees, elbows sticking out. 'Who do you think I'd help? People in the same boat as I was in.'

'Very interesting,' Randall said politely, but Knebworth hadn't finished yet.

'I had enough money and more to spare. So I founded *Missing*.' He gave a contented grin. 'That's how I met my wife. Her husband disappeared into thin air. Probably dead after causing a nasty crash which ended with a girl being disfigured and disabled.'

Randall broke in testily, 'But it isn't *your* life story I'm interested in, Mr Knebworth. You haven't had *your* throat cut.'

Something about the man's jaunty air was annoying him but his irritation didn't even seem to reach Knebworth. He just laughed.

'That's right,' he said good-naturedly, 'I haven't, have I? But I don't know how . . .?'

'The thick herringbone coat worn by our gentleman when he was killed together with some trousers. They came from your shop in Wyle Cop.'

'More than that,' Knebworth said, 'they came from me. They used to be mine.'

'Well, that answers another question,' Randall said. 'Had you left anything in the pockets?'

'Nah.'

'Or stitched into the lining?'

Again, Knebworth shook his head.

'Have you ever seen these before?' He produced the picture of the child's shoe and the four medals on their pin.

Knebworth looked at them for less than a minute then shook his head. 'I'm sorry,' he said, sounding genuine, 'they're nothing to do with me. It was just the coat and the trousers.'

Another blind alley, Randall was thinking as, twenty minutes later, he drove back down the perfectly straight, manicured drive.

Monday, 22 September, 10 a.m.

The CS had been summoned to Genevieve Dreyfuss's garden shed and began to turn it over, if not tear it apart piece by piece, practically plank by plank while she watched anxiously from the kitchen window. The phrase 'no stone unturned' would have applied to them. They were thorough and took everything out. Randall had instructed them that they were looking for a notebook or possibly sheets of paper. Even to find the pen would have been something. After his meeting with Knebworth, Randall himself visited the site and eyed the neat garden and the hive of activity. Then he spoke to the now distraught Miss Dreyfuss.

'Is there anywhere your gentleman could possibly have hidden an exercise book? Perhaps in the house?'

She looked baffled. 'Why would he want to?'

Randall couldn't answer this either.

Genevieve Dreyfuss looked even more upset. 'He never really came in the house,' she said, 'apart from to eat, and I was always here. I never saw him with an exercise book or writing anything.'

'When you were out did he have access to the inside?'

She shook her head and seemed a little embarrassed. 'It wasn't that I didn't trust him,' she protested and Randall sensed the 'but' . . .

It came. 'But I always locked up when I went out.' She tried to smile it off. 'Habit, I suppose. I have an outside toilet with a sink. I just left that open.'

Randall nodded. He was beginning to read between the lines. Oh, yes, people 'trusted' the hobos, but not that much.

He returned to the garden to watch the CS team at work. If there was anything here they would find it.

They didn't. But they did find the pen, cleverly slipped down the material where the sun lounger fabric loosely hugged the hollow tubing.

And Randall would bet a bottle of champagne that the insignificant biro was the one their man Charles had begged from Phoebe Walker at the *Missing* shop. He eyed it in the evidence bag and knew it would throw up bugger all in forensic evidence. It would give them nothing. Tell them nothing. But still, they had to go through the motions. It was evidence. Then his thoughts tracked elsewhere. It was a biro, worth less than a pound, and yet Charles, who had once been rich enough to afford a skiing holiday in Switzerland in the seventies, and had offered Phoebe a ten-pound note, had hoarded it like a Rolex watch. Randall's thoughts travelled further. Had Charles elected to become a vagrant or had it been forced on him through fear or debt? Which was it?

He returned to the station and the news that the coroner had left a message. Martha wanted to speak to him about setting a date for opening the inquest and their unknown man's burial.

He rang her back, feeling flat and disappointed. He had hoped that when eventually their man was either buried or cremated they would have a name, perhaps family or friends or business acquaintances – people to mourn him, bury him. For himself, he wanted the story of his past and his killer brought to justice. Instead he was faced with a plot number and an anonymous wooden cross.

But he knew Martha; she would want things tidied up. She wouldn't like the thought of a man's unidentified corpse lying *ad infinitum* in the mortuary fridge.

Martha sensed the disappointment in the detective's tone and kept the arrangements to a minimum. She'd already spoken to Mark Sullivan. The date of the funeral was set for Thursday October 23, three days after the inquest and six weeks after Charles had met his death.

'I'm sorry, Alex,' she said. 'I know that your part in this is far from over but I think it best if we open an inquest and bury him.'

'As you wish.' His voice was like lead, heavy with fallen hope.

Monday, 22 September, 9 p.m.

The briefing that evening was uninspired. DI Alex Randall was well aware that they were no further forward. They still did not know their man's name, neither did they have any idea who had killed him or why. It was all still a mystery. And now plans were being made to bury that mystery.

They'd gone over the few facts they knew but Randall wondered now whether to be buried in an unmarked grave would have been what Charles would have wanted. Perhaps it was the final unsatisfactory wish of this enigmatic man.

Randall feared that this would remain an unsolved mystery.

It wasn't a great thought and, looking round his fellow officers' faces, he knew that they were thinking the same thing.

They listened again to Delia Shaw's account of her encounter with Phoebe Walker. Randall and Dart described their contact with Sharp, Hook and John Hyde but again, none of them could extract anything useful from the encounters. They hadn't even learned anything useful from *Missing*'s founder, Graham Knebworth.

As the discussions continued, Randall was aware that the differing accounts of their man all matched. Polite, a gentleman, cultured. So where

190

had he come from? Was there any particular reason he had come to Shrewsbury? It looked as though he had arrived at Moreton Corbet by chance. That was where the lorry had been headed. Had it been going somewhere else he would have gone there. Had it been the rain that had made him take shelter in the castle cellar? He'd had nothing waterproof with him and the coat would soon have become saturated, heavy and cold. Had his real destination been somewhere else? Had his killer deliberately followed him there or happened upon him by chance?

And the pen. What had he been writing? Who had he been writing to? A letter? An account of his life and situation? Had that been such a threat that he had had to be killed? If it had been a letter, had it been that which had summoned the killer to him?

He batted the questions out to the waiting officers and watched them toss around the same ideas he had – that there had been some event in Charles's past that had caused him to escape his former identity. Nothing criminal or they would have had his prints and ID as quick as a snap of the fingers. No one resembling him was on their missing persons' database so no one had reported him missing.

And that had to be significant. No one had reported him missing.

Why not? Was there no one who missed him? Did this, he asked the team, mean that somewhere buried in Charles's past was some incident, some crime, some fear?

It was impossible to answer.

Randall was slightly irritated with himself. He should have been able to work something out from these random points. And yet he was still simply splashing around in shallow water, getting absolutely nowhere. And scanning the room full of the familiar faces of his team he could read only confusion there as well.

He handed the briefing over to Roberts and Talith, who spent some time describing to the team the scene at the gardening shed, each small detail helping to form a more complete, but still confusing, picture of their man. First of all, they described Miss Dreyfuss's expression of fondness for their vagrant before going on to describe the interior of the shed in detail, using photographs to illustrate their point of obsessive tidiness. Randall frowned. This was not the normal chaotic life of the homeless. It did not fit in with the usual man with mental illness or a drug or alcohol problem. He looked at the photographs, as did the rest of the team. These were the actions of a tidy man, someone methodical who disliked loose ends, someone who would not just disappear on a whim and stay hidden for years. Therefore the reason for his vagrancy and wanderings must also be reasoned, as was the motive behind his deliberate and carefully preserved anonymity. The man had been writing something. So, if this man had laid a trail of breadcrumbs it would lead somewhere. And now Randall believed that a link existed between the man's carefully concealed identity and his murder, which had not been a random attack either. Not a fists-and-feet beating up but that one deliberate, cruel, precise, fatal slash. It was hardly a large step to take that he had not been the unfortunate victim of a random assault but of a planned murder with a structured reason. Which meant, as his hitch-hike to Moreton Corbet had been chance, he must have been followed to the castle. What part did the castle play? Such a dramatic backdrop both in the physical and emotional sense, past and present. Had it been a deliberate setting? Had their murderer had a sense of the dramatic? *Yes.*

It was now ten o'clock. He switched his mobile phone back on and saw a missed call from Martha's home number. He rang back. 'I'm at home,' she said. 'Why don't you come over – have a spot of supper and a drink and I can tell you what I've learned this afternoon.'

It was too tempting an offer to refuse. He was on his way.

Twenty-Six

He arrived twenty minutes later. She'd opened a bottle of red wine and had some leftover lasagne ready to put in the microwave. Sam was out training and Sukey was socializing with friends. She was in the house on her own.

He accepted the offer of the lasagne and took a long sip of the wine.

'So,' she said, 'how did the briefing go?' She was perfectly aware that this was not how contacts between coroner and senior investigating officers were normally conducted. This was more pally, more friendly, more intimate – and she liked it.

'You first,' he said, eyes twinkling. 'You're the one that phoned. You tell me your bit.'

She would have said, *You show me yours and I'll show you mine*, but it had connotations and it was too dangerous a game to play. Instead she merely smiled. 'Have I ever mentioned my friend Miranda Mountford to you?'

'I think you have,' he said. 'Didn't she have a husband who was a nasty piece of work, threatening her? Violent?'

'That's the one,' she said. 'He's gone. Out of the picture. In South Africa, thank goodness. She's free of him.'

Randall took another sip of wine and dug his fork into the lasagne. He gave her an appraising look. 'Is that how women talk when they've shed a partner?' He was teasing her.

'It is when they're a nasty piece of work,' she said. Then added, 'Anyway, he's gone and that's good.'

Randall waited for her to get to the real point for this contact.

'She works part-time now,' she paused, 'in Public Health. The rest of the time she does charity work.'

'Ahh,' he said, on his way to understanding. 'Let me take a guess – at the charity.'

'You're right,' she said. 'And she knew him. She knew your man. She worked for *Missing*.'

He followed the same thought process as she'd done. 'Why didn't she come to us and tell us? We've asked anyone who knew him to come forward.'

'She did. But she couldn't give any information because she didn't know any facts – only what he was like. What sort of person he was.'

'Which was?'

'Polite, well spoken, not a drug addict or a drunk. Just a nice guy.'

'So where did he come from, this nice guy, this person who takes such trouble to tell no one his name, this person who gets his throat cut? Why did he have to remain such an enigma? Why is he still an enigma? Why was it so important to him? Was it the discovery of his identity that led to his murder? To be honest, Martha, I want to know that as much as I want to know who held the knife.'

'We may never find out,' Martha pointed out. 'Have you thought of that?'

Randall nodded, meeting her eyes.

'There was something else, Alex. On occasions she saw him writing.'

Now he was listening.

'Having begged a pen from the girl who worked at the *Missing* shop.'

'Yes – we've found the pen. PC Shaw spoke to the girl in the shop. Do we have any clue what he was writing? Was it sheets of paper? A letter? A notebook?'

'An exercise book which he would pocket if anyone tried to look.'

To Randall, writing meant information. Perhaps Charles was reluctant to tell people who he was but not so reluctant to write things down. His life story was somewhere. He felt excited.

'We've found no exercise book, Martha,' he said steadily. 'And the CS boys have practically demolished the garden shed. There's nothing there and no exercise book was found on the body.'

'Did he work for anyone else apart from your Miss Dreyfuss?'

'No one else has come forward so far.' He fell silent and she jumped to her role in the case, leapfrogging over his own thought processes.

'It's time we buried him, Alex. We can't leave him in the mortuary fridge for ever.'

Randall nodded. 'Yes.' Then he started to tell her a bit more about Genevieve Dreyfuss's shed. He showed her a picture of the interior and she looked across at him, puzzled.

'But this doesn't make any sense,' she said. 'This man is obsessional. How could he be a vagrant, a tramp? Unwashed in dirty clothes that were someone else's?'

'I don't know.'

'It's almost like a disguise,' she said slowly.

Randall looked at her. 'I would have thought that myself. But for five years?'

They both heaved a sigh. Then he moved on to tell her that they had tracked down the origin of the coat.

'And you think this man, Knebworth, knows something about our man?'

'I don't know, Martha . . .' He'd finished the lasagne and now took a last sip of the wine. 'He seemed kosher when PC Shaw and I visited him. He knew our man. Talked to him, seemed to like him but he couldn't really tell us anything more.' He leaned across the table and put his hand over hers. 'Thank you,' he said, 'for the information. Somewhere,' he said, 'our man has penned his story.'

'And hidden it.'

'If we find it we'll learn his story. If we don't he'll remain an enigma. But where could he have hidden it?'

'The obvious place would have been in the shed.'

'Yes,' he agreed. 'Miss Dreyfuss told us she never went in there.'

'But you say it can't be there?'

Randall shook his head. 'Not a chance,' he said. 'The CS boys are thorough.'

They were both silent, then Randall recalled something. 'There is something more,' he said, 'but it's probably not going to help.'

'Go on.'

'PC Coleman found a young lad amongst the homeless who was apparently familiar with our friend,' He smiled at her. 'I quote, "He used to talk in his sleep."'

Martha was leaning forward in her eagerness to hear this. Talking in his sleep, to her, sounded like unguarded statements.

'What did he say?'

'Again, I quote.' Randall used the jottings he had on his iPad. 'Stuff like he'd scream and say "*not you*" and then he'd say "*splash*". And then, "*Take the money. Have it. Have it all.*" Then, "*Knock, knock, knock, I must finish these shoes.*" And then . . .' He hesitated. '"*One hundred and five, north tower*,"' he said, frowning. 'It all sounded like nonsense to me, the ramblings of a disturbed mind.'

'The ramblings,' she said, 'of an unguarded mind. We all know that in our dreams our true feelings come out.'

Randall stared at her. The coroner was looking on these *ramblings* as important. He continued more slowly. 'The boy wrongly deduced that Charles had been in prison.'

'Or the army,' Martha said. 'The medals?'

Randall shook his head. 'It wasn't possible he'd been awarded the medals himself,' he said. 'He wouldn't have been born. And almost certainly neither was his father, unless he was elderly when he fathered Charles.'

'Grandfather,' Martha said slowly. 'Many people idolize their grandparents.' She warmed to her point. 'Mine, for instance . . .' She smiled.

'I idolize mine. Sorry,' she apologized. 'I'm veering off the subject, aren't I?'

Randall nodded. 'Maybe another time.'

'I don't suppose your young vagrant said if Charles ever spoke a name?'

'Yeah. Lucy. Our friend tells us he cried it a couple of times in his sleep but when he woke him up and asked him who Lucy was he said he looked blank and that he didn't know anyone called Lucy.'

'Lucy,' she considered thoughtfully.

Randall recovered something else. 'Funny thing is, Martha, that Phoebe, the girl from the charity shop, told PC Shaw he called her Lucy too.'

'A daughter, I wonder?' she mused.

'Perhaps.'

'But wouldn't a daughter have reported her father's disappearance?'

'Yes.'

'So, even with this added, random information, you still don't know who he is?'

He confided in her then, that this was the way Charles wanted it.

'We'll stick to our planned dates for the inquest and then his burial.'

He nodded, shoulders bowed as though he felt a failure. Martha wanted to say something but she couldn't find the right words. Everything she thought of seemed fatuous and he would soon sense that any statement, however encouraging it was meant to be – that they would soon find out who their man was, who had killed him and why – would be very obviously hollow, untrue and pointless.

So after a few pleasantries Randall stood up and Martha saw him to the door. Almost without considering what he had been about to do, as he wished her goodnight, he bent, pushed aside the tangle of red hair and kissed her cheek.

Then he was gone.

Leaving Martha motionless. But it wasn't only the kiss. Something was pricking her memory.

As she stood there, car headlights swung into the drive. Sam was home and he'd picked Sukey up from town.

Oh, the joy of mobile phone communication.

Now the house was filled with noise and light and whatever it was that had given her a spark of realization now abandoned her.

Twenty-Seven

Monday, 20 October, 10.30 a.m.

She sat and surveyed the room. She had hoped
that holding an inquest might provide some
answers, publicize their man's murder, maybe
flush someone out who would come forward or
proffer a comment or information that would help
them ID the man. But instead it was a dry affair
with John Hyde detailing the circumstances of
the discovery of the body, Randall giving the
bare bones of the police investigation and Mark
Sullivan describing the findings of the post-
mortem. He mentioned the fact that the prosthesis
had been numbered and the patient's ID would
have been recorded but that the hospital in
Switzerland was having trouble locating the
records of the injury and data on the patient who
had had the prosthesis inserted.

From being a promising lead it had, so far,
shrivelled into nothing.

Alex Randall had finished by saying that the
police investigation was ongoing and that they
would be following up all their leads.

Martha had no option but to pronounce a verdict
of homicide by person or persons unknown and
to set the date of the funeral for the Thursday of
that week. She used the opportunity to make
another public appeal for anyone who knew or

201

thought they knew their man or anything about the crime itself to contact either her or the police at Monkmoor station. 'We are very anxious,' she said in her clear voice, 'to ascertain this man's identity so he can be buried with dignity under his real name. At the same time the police are investigating a savage and cruel murder and have few leads to go on. There is a possibility that the assailant might strike again. Until we understand why this crime happened, who our victim is and who the perpetrator is we can only give this person an unknown grave. This is obviously a travesty which we wish to reverse as soon as possible. This man deserves the dignity of his identity. Thank you. The inquest is adjourned pending further police investigation.'

She stood up and the court stood up with her. Jericho was clipping together a sheaf of papers in the front. As her assistant he was always in the court to hear cases. Part of his job was to collect witnesses. In this case there were precious few. None, really.

23 October was a Thursday and the burial was arranged for eleven a.m. The day of the funeral was suitably sombre, a grey day, cold, the traditional words of the committal muffled by thick fog. Appropriate for someone who had shrouded his own life and past in similarly thick fog. Alex and Mark had turned up together with a few of the investigating team and they stood, a scatter of personnel and representatives of the press with their unmistakable long lenses and recording equipment. Martha stood by the open grave trying not to recall the day she had buried Martin while

Vera looked after the two-year-old twins. It had been a day very much like this one, damp, drizzly, depressing. She reflected, was it worse to bury a loved one on a bright cheerful day as though their loss was being celebrated? Or, if you were a Christian, perhaps it was their ascent into heaven which was being celebrated. Or was it better to say goodbye on a day such this when death seemed like the very end of the world? A most terrible and painful eternal goodbye?

She drew in a deep sigh and focused on the day's events. No good living in the past. She'd done that for long enough.

Charles's plot would be marked by a plot number and she wondered whether he would, one day, be exhumed. Would they ever know who he was or would he remain forever anonymous? Known unto God. She closed her eyes. There were so many phrases for it. Known unto God. The Unknown Warrior. The Tomb of the Unknown Soldier, the thousands of people's body parts who never had the dignity of this. Ruanda, the Congo, Sudan, Syria, Iraq, the Ukraine, 9/11 . . . the list was endless. She glanced across at Alex Randall and wondered what he was thinking. He met her eyes but instead of smiling or nodding or even looking away he seemed to be peering right into her heart.

Don't go there, Alex.

It was she who broke the gaze, feeling her face flush as only a redhead's can. She wasn't sure she wanted Detective Inspector Alex Randall peering right into her soul. But in that brief look she knew he felt a failure, disappointed that he had not yet made an arrest and disappointed in his own unhappy personal life. She would have liked to have put her hand in his.

Walk on.

The committal was brief, the words pared to a bare minimum, just enough to give their man dignity. The coffin was plain pine, the cheapest in the range, the brass plate simply saying unknown man, the date and whereabouts of his murder and an identification number. It would be useful if they did exhume him as the undertakers would be the ones to identify the coffin. The plot would be marked with a simple white wooden cross. Nothing fancy for Mr Nobody.

Martha murmured a brief prayer of her own, not only the usual rest in peace, but also a pledge that they would not rest until they had found his killer. She never made promises she could not keep and so resisted the temptation to promise that they would find his killer – even to herself. They might not. Ever.

On the other side of the grave stood the rest of the investigating team, their heads bowed, hands clasped, respectful. There were a few members of the public. She recognized Gilbert Warrilow from English Heritage and a small cluster of people she imagined were the inhabitants of Moreton Corbet. One was a sulky looking but glamorous blonde who shuffled on unsuitable heels from foot to foot, impatient to be somewhere else or simply uncomfortable. And right on the edge of the cluster of people, to her delight, she recognized Miranda with a man in jeans and thick white hair. She gave them both a swift smile. It would not do for the coroner to be seen smiling at an unknown's funeral.

Right at the back of the graveyard stood four of the homeless, heads also bowed, shuffling away from the grave already. They'd paid their respects.

She was aware of Alex Randall turning to face her and his hand moved involuntarily towards her so she knew he felt the same as she did. To be able to hold hands would have brought comfort to them both.

'Thank you for being here,' he mouthed over the well-known words.

'We flourish like a flower of the field; when the wind goes over it, it is gone and its place will know it no more.'

Never had the phrases sounded so poignant.

Martha repeated the words to herself. *When the wind goes over it, it is gone and its place will know it no more.* The words rang in her brain, jangling, discordant, almost a warning: *And its place will know it no more.* She had a picture of a man sliding into a quicksand which closed over his head so completely it seemed to her not only that *its place would know it no more*, but rather it was as though its place had never been.

The man who never was.

As the soil rattled on the coffin she walked straight across to DI Randall. 'It isn't the end, you know, Alex,' she said.

He looked bleak. 'It just feels like it.'

'Will you be winding down your investigation?'

'Not yet. But the time will come, you know. Like it or not.'

Miranda, dressed in black trousers and jacket, had approached them. With a hugely flirtatious smile, she held her hand out to the detective. 'You must be Alex,' she said with a grin as wide as the bloody Mississippi. 'I've heard so much about you.'

Martha felt her lips tighten and shot her friend a furious scowl. How dare she.

Alex was discomforted. 'Umm,' he said, and looked to Martha for a cue.

She took the challenge smoothly. 'If she heard it from me it would all be extremely bad,' she said, shooting a grin now at her friend. 'So don't worry, Alex.'

He entered into the spirit of things. 'Then I won't,' he said, still a little stiff and uncomfortable in Knebworth's presence, whom he hadn't quite crossed off his list of suspects.

Knebworth, for his part, was perfectly comfortable. 'And you must be our coroner,' he said to Martha. She smiled and nodded.

'We're just going to go for something to eat,' Miranda said to both Martha and Alex, not in the least abashed. 'Will you join us?'

'Umm,' he said again.

Twenty-Eight

Thursday, 30 October, 11 a.m.

It was a week after the funeral that Martha's brain finally clicked into gear and it was as though the cog had found its forward motion. She could not think why or how she had not put two and two together before and realized why the phrases spoken by their unknown man in his sleep had sounded so familiar. Her subconscious must have been wrestling on with the problem all this time. She took a book from the bookshelf to check. And knew she had been right.

She picked up the phone and rang Alex Randall's extension number. To her frustration it was put straight through to answerphone. Almost breathless with excitement she left her name, the time and date of the call and asked that he ring her back as soon as he received her message.

It was hard to focus on her work with something like a wasp buzzing around in her brain. She wanted to ring again but knew there was no point. The detective inspector was not available.

An hour and a half went by, Martha by now frantically impatient. Finally, at twelve thirty, the phone rang.

'Martha.' Alex's voice. 'Whatever is it? You sounded almost fizzing with excitement.'

207

'I was.'

'So what is it?'

'Can you come over?'

'Now?'

'Yes.'

He laughed. 'This very minute?'

He was teasing her again. Oh, Alex. It reminded her so much of Martin. He would use that same light tone to gently tease what he saw as her red-headed passions.

'OK,' he said, giving in. 'I'm on my way.' He couldn't resist one last leg-pull. 'Do I need to put the blue light on?'

Two could play at that game. 'If you like.'

He chuckled and put the phone down.

Twenty minutes later he was knocking at her door.

Jericho was having to get used to the intrusions of the DI who had greeted him, told him the coroner had summoned him this time and climbed the stairs, long legs two at a time.

Martha didn't even try to hide her excitement. 'I think I'm close to understanding Charles's obscure references,' she said.

'Oh?'

'I think he was a shoemaker,' she said.

Alex Randall sank down into the chair, his eyes fixed on her. 'How on earth do you come by that?'

'We had clues,' she said. 'The shoe?'

'Ye-es?'

'One hundred and five, north tower. Your home-less man who heard him talking in his sleep thought he must have been in prison. But he couldn't have been or you'd have had a record of his fingerprints. DNA.'

Randall nodded cautiously. Warily.

She ploughed on. 'And didn't he call the girl in the charity shop Lucy?'

Again, Randall nodded, still with the same caution, but frowning now.

She handed him a book. Randall looked at it.

'Have you read it?'

'Ages ago,' he said.

'Do you remember a character in it called Doctor Manette? A man wrongly imprisoned in the Bastille who takes up a shoemaking hobby?'

'Hobby?' He was startled. But it was one way of putting it.

'He has a daughter called Lucy. And in the Bastille he was forgotten about. Anonymous as though he was dead. He wrote a letter denouncing the person responsible for his imprisonment.'

Alex Randall was speechless.

'I know this book well,' she continued. 'One Hundred and Five, North Tower refers to his prison cell.' She said the words with a shiver before explaining her familiarity with the classic. 'Sukey was in a production of *A Tale of Two Cities* last year.' She leafed through her copy. 'The part she played,' she said, 'was the daughter of Doctor Alexandre Manette, Lucy.'

'Sukey?' he queried.

'My daughter. Eighteen and now studying to be an actress.'

'Really? That's an interesting career choice.'

'Not mine,' she said, holding her hands up. 'I didn't say anything to her about being an actress.

209

She just chose it. I don't know where it came from.'

'And your son?' He knew she had twins: a girl and a boy.

'Sam – well, he's playing football at the moment but there's another shock.' She hunched her shoulders up. 'He now says he just wants to do this for a few more years and then train as a teacher. Kids,' she said in mock exasperation.

'I envy you,' he said. 'They sound wonderful. Just wonderful.'

'And like the completely biased mother that I am,' she said, laughing, 'I heartily agree. Now then, we both need to act as detectives in this, don't we?'

He nodded. 'That's what I came for.'

She was smiling now. He was the detective, not she.

'So we need to pool our knowledge about the man we've been calling Charles,' she said. 'Everyone describes him as polite, private, reticent. He wasn't a drunk or a drug addict.'

Randall shook his head.

Martha continued, 'You've had Mark's toxicology report as well. That supports that. He was clean.'

'Yes.'

'We think he was well educated and at some point in his life he had the money to go on a skiing holiday.'

'Ye-es,' Randall agreed tentatively, not quite sure where all this was leading.

'He made veiled references to having had two lives.'

210

Randall leaned forward, listening hard.

'He said he was already dead.'

'Yes.' He could not but agree.

'And he's been on the road for somewhere around five years.'

'Again, yes. But what does this tell us?'

She held a finger up. 'Patience, Alex. I don't know it all. I'm just throwing everything we know about him into the melting pot. Just to refresh your memory,' she continued, her eyes sparkling, 'Doctor Manette wrote down an account of his trials,' she said, 'of the injustice that was done to him. He hid it in a hole in a chimney where a stone had been worked out and replaced.'

Alex Randall was staring at her. 'Moreton Corbet,' he breathed.

'Then what are we waiting for?'

Twenty-Nine

It took them twenty long minutes to reach Moreton Corbet Castle, still closed to the public and with an officer on guard. Not for much longer. They would be winding down the investigation now that the inquest and funeral were over. Surely, Randall had reasoned, they had collected all the evidence? But as he parked in the lay-by and Martha climbed out, he wondered.

Signs of the murder were almost gone but not quite. Flowers had been laid. Quite a lot considering no one knew who their victim was. Martha scanned some of the cards as she passed.

We don't know who you are. We don't know why you died but you are in our thoughts.

Unknown man. We are sorry.

You are not a nobody.

We will pray for you. This one signed by the Vicar and Congregation of Moreton Corbet Church.

And a slightly puzzling one considering the circumstances: *Tell us who you are.*

Then there was the one that always surfaced in such circumstances: The ubiquitous *why?*

There was still police tape denying access to the general public and the site was deserted apart from the one solitary PC who was now striding towards them.

Alex turned to Martha, supressing a smile. 'Do

212

you think, if we're going to vandalize this place we should at least run it past English Heritage?'

She shot him a frustrated look before realizing that he was, again, teasing her.

He greeted the young PC and they opened the gate. 'Right, so where?'

But Martha had stopped, almost out of respect. 'It's such a place, she said. 'It has such an air of tragedy. It almost seems fitting that a murder should happen here.' She turned to face him. 'I wouldn't be surprised if it's not the first.'

She was right. It was a ruin you could not ignore but, anxious to get on with the job, Randall simply nodded and moved forward.

'OK, clever clogs,' Randall said, not looking at the ruined house now but at her flushed, eager face. 'So where now?'

'Well . . .' Martha stepped over the grass. 'Didn't you say Charles was found in the cellar?'

'Yeah, over here.' Randall's long legs were already taking him across the lawns, heading towards the main facade. 'And here is the dining chamber . . .'

Martha was struggling to keep up with him as they scrambled over the stones. 'So here . . .' she was now standing in front of what must once have been a fireplace, '. . . is where the chimney would have been.'

They stood in front of it. 'Remember the words,' Martha reminded him. 'In a hole, in the chimney, where a stone had been worked out and replaced.'

They had thought it would be easier but they spent almost forty-five minutes pulling and wriggling stones before Alex found one that yielded to his fingers. He hardly control his excitement. 'Martha,' he said, urgency in his tone. 'I think I've found it.' He pulled and a large stone came tumbling out, behind it a hole containing a child's exercise book.

They were both dying to touch it but Randall knew the rules and slipped some gloves on before leafing through a couple of the pages. 'I think it's all going to be here,' he said and placed it in an evidence bag.

He summoned the police officer, who took photographs of the site where the book had been pulled from and pointed out, 'Something else here, sir.'

He pulled out the very same edition of the very same book that Martha had had in the office.

A Tale of Two Cities by Charles Dickens, Macmillan and Co., Limited, St Martin's Street, London. And underneath the date of this edition: 1945. The year the Second World War had ended.

The drive back to the station was as frustrating as the drive out had been. They were both dying to read their man's notes, to finally know his name, to find out his fate, and there was now a distinct possibility that they would discover the identity of his killer.

And so, in Alex's area of the office, they finally read the story of the man they had half-mockingly, half-pityingly called Charles.

And the first thing they read was a name. But their tramp did not disclose all straight away. He held them on a string.

This is my confession. As a true Catholic it is important to me that I make it not only to a priest. My name is Ishmael, only it isn't. We all know Ishmael is Melville's wandering whaler so no. I am not he. You will know my name in time. My great-grandfather came from Holland in the late nineteenth century. Already skilled as a shoe-maker. Martha shot a triumphant glance at Alex.

Yes, shoes and shoemakers. So many in litera-ture, their man mused. *The Brothers Grimm's 'The Elves and the Shoemaker'. Cinderalla's glass slipper. The slippers you wear which will dance you to death. Moira Shearer's Red Shoes – the shoes that fit. And the most poignant of all, Doctor Manette's 105 North Tower and the shoe-makers' bench which he could not bear to be parted from and turned to in times of crisis. Shoes for a lady, shoes for a man – for a fine man. My great-grandfather made shoes for all kinds, ladies and gentlemen, but the shoes he was most proud of he gave away. They were clogs for children that had no shoes. And he made them just as carefully. One little girl wore them and then gave them back. She said she had nothing else to give him as a thank-you present and so she took them off her feet, hardly worn, and presented them to him. My great-grandfather was touched. He talked about the widow's mite and when his factory expanded and became hugely successful and he a millionaire many times over he preserved the shoes in a glass case to remind him. They were, he said, the most precious gift he had ever received. The child had walked away barefoot because she wanted to give him a present. She* had given him all she had. Needless to say, he brought the child back and, put it like this: her life was not poor after that.

She eventually married my grandfather.

My grandfather and then my father and later myself joined the business, still making leather shoes and boots. The factory did well then. We were exporting to many countries long before this was common practice. We expanded but did not over- expand. The factory made soldiers' boots throughout both wars and provided uniform boots and shoes in the years between. You might have seen my set of medals. More about those later.

I married a girl called Verity, which is a laugh as the name means truth. She was a dancer and we had been considering whether to branch out into dancers' shoes. Pointe shoes. They are always uncomfortable and hurt and damage dancers' feet, giving them all sorts of problems later on in life. My father, who loved the ballet, was unhappy about this and spent many years researching into Pointe shoes. He came up with a new design and I went to the ballet school to see what the dancers thought of them, and that was how I met Verity. We were married in the year 2000 when she was just eighteen years old. I was thirty. But we were happy for a few years until roughly 2008. You know how these things are. It is hard to put your finger on one particular day and say that is the day it started to go wrong but certainly by the end of 2009 I was aware that something was very wrong. I do not need to go into detail yet.

We had many friends, amongst whom was a man called Rafael Poulson. I don't know how he became one of our circle of friends. He liked boats and said he'd been in the military like his father and grandfather before him. Another family business, he joked. I didn't even think Verity liked him. But perhaps dancers can be actresses too. I never saw her speak to him but he was apparently one of our friends. Suddenly there he was.

I move forward to 2010, March. A cold and blustery day. Poulson and I had fallen into the habit of sailing from Chichester, just taking trips around the bay, you know. Boy stuff, Verity used to call it. Sometimes she would come with us. Sometimes not. That evening she did come. The water was rough so I was surprised. She had a delicate – hah – constitution and often used to say she felt very sick on boats. That night is still hazy, like a bad dream, as though my mind wants to protect me from its ugliness. I wanted to turn back but Rafael did not. He loved the adventure and he was a competent sailor. No doubt about that. I did feel safe with him at the helm. Right up to when he crashed the boom around and struck me on the head. Verity was standing behind him and to my shock she was encouraging him. No, not encouraging – goading him into killing me. Her face was villainous. Evil. And she actually grabbed the boom and hit me again so I fell into the water. But the sail had swung with the boom, catching the wind, and the boat capsized. I lay in the water without the volition to swim or even try to float. I was puzzling over what had happened. My wife wanted me dead? And the last image I had was of her face, hating me.

As I lay, somehow not drowning in the water, I thought of my life. Under my hand the once thriving business had become shaky. Four generations on, what was I going to achieve? My father had died two years before and I had grieved for him. He had been a good man and I missed him, which explains why I suppose I took my finger off the button as far as my marriage and the business went. So the business was failing and my wife wanted to kill me.

Martha looked up. 'What a sad story.'

Randall nodded, his eyes focused on the neat writing, ignoring the officers who were glancing across, curious.

She continued reading. *I was picked up by a boat but they were Dutch drug runners and didn't know what to do with me, and to be honest I didn't really care. I just sat, catatonic. Even depression wouldn't describe it. I felt hollow. Dead. I didn't want to be me anymore. They were talking about what to do with me in Dutch and I had picked up a little of what they were saying. The BBC World Service was on the radio and through it I learned my fate. Or not. I heard my name spoken in one of the bulletins. I heard that a body washed ashore had been identified by 'his' wife (my wife) as the missing yachtsman, Simeon van Helsing, the shoe multi-millionaire. They announced the date and time of his funeral. My funeral. So there you have it. I was no longer officially alive. I was dead and about to be buried.*

What irony that the drowned corpse could not be me but her 'also missing' lover.

In the end, after six or seven days, they tossed me over the side of the boat, thinking, I suppose, that as I was so apathetic and half-dead that I would not attempt to swim but simply drown. Or maybe they didn't really care what happened to me. But the human spirit is strong. I could not prevent my arms and legs from making the motions that would keep me afloat. I could not force myself to drown and so I swam ashore. I did return in the night to the factory and took one of the precious little shoes out of the glass case. And then I remembered. It had been raining once and Poulson had lent me his mac. It still hung in my office. I had forgotten to return it. In the pocket were the medals he so proudly flourished on every conceivable occasion. I knew it had been a lie. And so I had these two objects to remind me of the very best and worst of human nature. I vowed I would keep them with me. From my drawer I took my copy of A Tale of Two Cities, *a book I had always loved because of its connection with shoemaking. I remembered that my life had been insured for a million pounds. And now Verity would have it. Could have it. If I had just been declared missing she would have had to wait for the obligatory seven years. But Verity did not like to wait for anything. She had the impatience of the young woman she still was. She would want her money* now. *I could hear her petulant voice. So there is your story and my story. Verity was the only winner to the tragedy and a newspaper I read a day or two later told me her fate too. She, somehow, had managed to inflate the life raft and had been found shivering and cold but alive. My poor little dancing sparrow.*

I decided that as I was dead I was released from my obligation to both business and wife. I had made a mess of both anyway. And now I had the freedom to choose the path I wanted. Life on the road appealed to me. No baggage. No wife to return to, no business, no family. It was better for everyone if I remained dead.

And so I found Shrewsbury, in Shropshire. A small town where I felt both comfortable and safe and I shed all obligations, everything that was part of my previous life, apart from the treasured little girl's shoe, (the girl who became my grandmother, did I say?), my book and the set of medals that had belonged to Poulson. It would remind me of the futility of inheritance. Of the deceit of so-called friends. And, ironically, I knew about Jane Kamara and her husband's disappearance. It seemed fitting to use Mr Knebworth's coat.

But a few months ago as I was sitting, reading on a bench in The Quarry, someone walked by. I don't know who he was. He was blonde and stocky, around my age, a man with a casual air, wearing a very expensive suit, and instead of walking by he stopped and stared at me. I stared back at the stranger, wondering why I commanded such scrutiny. After a while, without speaking to me, he walked on.

A week later, he was back. Same place – and staring at me again. Then he bent over me. 'I know who you are,' he said. 'You're not dead, are you?'

I admit I was nervous. I didn't know what to do except to write down all that had happened. I took courage and inspiration from Doctor Manette's actions.

He had survived. So could I.

But where to go?

Thinking about it, I am unnerved by that man. He knows who I am. What, I wonder, will he do with that knowledge? Should I, like a true hobo, move elsewhere, take to the road, find a new place?

This is what I will do. Move on.

But I will leave my account somewhere. And if you are reading this you must have found it. How? Why? Has something happened to me? Have you just been lucky? Or intuitive? Which is it? Tonight I shall not sleep in the field with the others. I shall take to the road. Go someplace else, wherever fate wills. Somewhere where I will not be found. I say goodbye to my friend, Miss Dreyfuss. I thank her for being my friend. I thank all who have been kind to me in my strange life.

Finally, I sign my name.

Simeon van Helsing

Martha looked up. 'Except he was found, wasn't he? I wonder who this man was who recognized him.'

Randall was already pressing keys.

Thirty

Friday, 31 October, Hallowe'en

Martha gave DI Randall twenty-four hours before she called him. She knew he would have work to do piecing together their man's story and, hopefully, tracking down his killer. None of this involved her. She would only be a distraction. She only hoped that the discovery of their man's identity would lead to an arrest.

But finally she picked up the phone.

'Martha,' he said, sounding truly glad to hear from her. 'I was just about to ring you. I've had an email from a dentist in Chalfont St Giles, just a bit puzzled that the dental records we circulated of our murdered man appear to match those of a person recorded as already dead.'

'Confirmation then.'

'Yes. It would appear so.' He paused. 'Is there any chance you can come over to the station?'

'OK,' she said, and was there in twenty minutes.

She found Alex Randall sitting in front of a computer screen. He looked up as she entered and grinned at her. The warmth in that grin took her aback.

'Thanks to you,' he said, 'I've got it all here. An account of the sailing accident. Naturally Poulson never was found.'

'Well, he was in a way,' she pointed out. 'It's

just that he was buried under Simeon van Helsing's name.'

'What about his family?'

'Apparently he didn't have close family. A mother who lived abroad who doesn't seem to have made much of the fact that her son had apparently drowned. A brother who inserted something in the Deaths column of the local newspaper. The family just appear to have accepted his "still missing, presumed drowned" status. Sad,' she said, 'even though he was a nasty piece of work.'

'Yes,' Randall agreed. 'And there's plenty of information about the Van Helsing Shoe Company, who appear to have gone from strength to strength.' He paused. 'They're now worth almost three billion pounds.'

'Under whose directorship?'

'Can't you guess?'

'Verity,' she said. 'But how come it's worth so much?'

'Handmade shoes for the wealthy. They keep foot measurements for the stars and have branched out into dance shoes, ballet, tap. Here,' he said. 'It's all here.'

Martha peered into the screen. No doubt about it: the Van Helsing Shoe Company was a thriving and successful business.

'So what now?'

'We're going to find it very difficult to convict Verity,' he said, 'who inherited something like sixteen million pounds from her husband's estate as well as the million from her husband's life insurance. She must have quite a talent for business to have turned it around so successfully. But according to their website she's worked hard, sourcing the leather and other products from abroad but all the manufacturing is done here, in this country. She employs over a thousand people.'

'Has she remarried?'

'It doesn't look like it. There's no mention of a husband.'

'Children?'

'No mention of those either.'

'Where does she live?'

'The Chalfonts,' he said. 'Just an hour's drive from London.'

'Have you contacted her?'

'Not yet.' He gave her another mischievous grin. 'I thought you'd like to be in on the action.'

Martha tried to keep her face straight, impassive and unenthusiastic – and failed completely.

'Even better than that,' Randall said, peering intently into the computer, 'I think this is our killer.'

Martha looked over his shoulder.

He was a beefy-looking blonde man with a cocky, confident gaze. Underneath was his name, Hiram Schumacher, described as thirty-five years old, ambitious and competent, with a degree from the University of London in Business Management. In his spare time he was into fencing, boxing and keeping fit.

Martha met Randall's eyes. 'You think?'

Randall nodded. 'He fits the profile. Call it instinct but I can just see him and Verity cosying up to one another.

'This guy is one of their executives. We're going to have to be very cautious,' he said. 'And as for Mrs Van Helsing, she'll be able to afford the very best defence counsel.' He looked at Martha. 'We have nothing to charge her with.'

'What about a false insurance claim? Wrongful identification of her husband?'

'She'll say she was so traumatized she made a mistake. The CPS won't buy it.' He was still looking at her. 'I can tell you that already.'

She nodded.

'She may well have had nothing to do with her husband's murder,' Randall said.

'But she was quite happy for him to be murdered five years ago. She was part of the plot. Probably initiated it.'

'Again, the only two people who could have given witness to that are both dead.'

'Maybe that's why, once discovered, he had to die. In case he re-surfaced.' She remembered a phrase from the Dickens. 'In case he was "recalled to life".'

Alex Randall nodded. 'It was always a possibility. But having seen his throat injury, unless she's built like a shot putter I can't see her inflicting the fatal wound. It was vicious and would have taken extreme force.'

'Well, we have a description of our assailant.'

But Randall shook his head. 'No, we don't,' he said. 'What's more, we haven't got any forensic evidence of him. All we have is *the notebook* with an account of our man's life. It will have to be proved that Van Helsing really did write it. And in it we have the description of a man who

225

appeared to recognize Simeon van Helsing. Nothing more. We can fingerprint it and try and match it up with a suspect, but we're going to have to prove it was Van Helsing's handwriting and that the notebook contains a true account of events. And then we're going to have to find some forensic evidence to support our theory. Unless we get a confession which, somehow, looking at this guy and knowing how much money's at stake, I very much doubt.'

She smiled. 'How quickly we've got used to calling him by his correct name.'

'Yes.'

She was thinking for a moment, trying to work things out. 'But surely in these days of surveillance, number plate recognition and so on, you can build up a case?'

'Hey.' Randall laughed. 'Hang on a minute. Who's the copper here? You're way ahead of me, Martha. A step at a time.' His eyes were warm as they rested on her. His look felt like a caress. 'Time I rang Mrs Verity van Helsing. Are you ready?'

She nodded. He picked up the phone and dialled, Martha sitting by his side, hardly daring to breathe, able to listen to just one side of the conversation.

'Hello, is that Verity van Helsing?'

A woman's voice responded cagily. She probably thought it was a cold call. Double glazing, solar panels or a mis-sold PPI.

'I'm Detective Inspector Alex Randall of Shrewsbury Police.'

There was a querying response.

'I wonder if I could come and talk to you, please.'

Another response. Martha fancied she heard a question in it. *What about?*

'I would prefer to talk to you face-to-face, Mrs Van Helsing, but I can tell you it concerns your late husband.'

There was another response, shriller this time, with a note of panic.

'Tomorrow?'

The response was one word. A submissive, *Yes.*

'I'll come to your house around eleven. Thank you.'

He put down the phone, met Martha's eyes, knew she would love to come. 'No,' he said gently. 'I can't jeopardize the case.'

And she had to accept it.

Thirty-One

The next day Martha was in such a state of tension she almost had a headache. She'd slept little during the night. Her mind had been full of the man's story, of the people involved and the double crime committed against Simeon van Helsing. When she did sleep it was light and fitful, her dreams a tangle of the Dickens story, of the Bastille, of a mansion in the Chalfonts, a sword flying through the air and a man's dying cry and all watched by what she now considered the repugnant and malevolent facade of Moreton Corbet Castle. At six she rose. She would get no more rest.

But work had to be done. She forced herself to plan the day ahead, to write letters, make phone calls, liaise with Jericho about dates for inquests and statements to some very persistent solicitors, but her heart was travelling down the M40 towards The Chalfonts.

Randall took Paul Talith with him to interview Verity van Helsing. On the way down he explained to his DS how Martha had helped in discovering their 'tramp's' hiding place for his message. Even as he spoke he felt a sense of pride in her. She astonished him with her lively, clever interest in the cases they had jointly been involved in.

Talith gave him a shrewd glance as though he

read what he was saying and also what he was not saying. He had his own private thoughts. The coroner was a beautiful woman, was clever and was also a widow. But his inspector? Talith took a surreptitious glance across. He didn't know. Married? He never mentioned a wife. Children? He didn't mention those either.

They turned off the motorway. The Chalfonts was a leafy area less than an hour from London, yet the scattered villages had the feeling of deepest countryside. Verity van Helsing lived in a large country house behind locked gates, accessible via a speakerphone. Randall gave Talith a look, stepped out of the car and spoke curtly into it. 'Detective Inspector Alex Randall for Mrs Van Helsing,' he said, and the gates swung open.

Back in the car, Talith turned to his DI. 'How the hell are you going to do this, boss?'

'I haven't quite worked it out, Talith. I thought I'd begin by asking her about her husband's "accident".'

'Well, best of luck with that one,' was Talith's response.

'What I'm really after,' Randall mused, 'is our killer. And I don't think that's going to be our Mrs van Helsing. She is a little more subtle than that and I don't think she'd have had the physical strength to strike the fatal blow. I have an idea but, as you know, Talith, an idea is hardly a conviction.'

'I wonder, sir, if it might be an idea to visit the factory then?'

'We can do that after we've spoken to our lady,'

Randall said. 'Perhaps Verity van Helsing herself would like to give us a tour.'

The front door opened as they reached the top of the drive and a woman stood there. Apart from saying that Van Helsing's wife would have to be built like a shot putter to have inflicted his fatal injury, Randall hadn't given Mrs Van Helsing's physical appearance any thought at all. He'd seen her picture on the factory website but it had been head and shoulders only and he had gained the impression of a hard face. Little else. Company portraits tended not to reveal much of a person. She had been a dancer so he had guessed at a small size. Certainly the woman who stood on the door step was that, trim and petite, a very beautiful woman somewhere in her thirties with a lovely bone structure, shining, beautiful blonde hair and big eyes as blue as the ocean. By his side, Talith gave a low whistle. 'Wow,' he said.

Mrs Van Helsing moved forwards with the grace of a panther. Yes, she still had a dancer's body and ease and grace of movement, poised and confident. Randall's next thought was treacherous: what a waste to send this woman to prison.

For what? Complicity to murder – not once but probably twice. He gritted his teeth, hardened his heart and held out his hand.

She appraised him coolly and Randall had to remind himself that this was also the woman who had turned the Van Helsing Shoe Company from a failing, probably old-fashioned, traditional family business into a clever multi-billion pound industry. He shook her hand.

'Now,' she said briskly, still on the doorstep.

'What is all this about? I don't know if you're aware but my husband died five years ago in a tragic sailing accident. One of his closest friends died with him.'

Talith gave the DI a swift glance.

'Yes,' Randall said. 'I've read the *accounts* of the tragedy. I believe you were in the boat too.'

It was at this point that Verity decided to invite them in.

She did so with reluctance and led them into a chintzy room, waving them towards a sofa and asking a young foreign girl to serve tea. She did not ask them whether they would prefer coffee. She would obviously go so far and no farther.

She sat opposite them, elegant in white trousers and a black top, crossed her legs and spoke. 'Am I to understand you're re-investigating my husband's death?'

It was the perfect opening.

'Indeed we are,' Randall said with a bland smile.

Verity licked her lips – the only sign, so far, of any nervousness.

The tea arrived and she bought herself time by pouring it, enquiring whether they wanted milk and sugar, passing the cups around.

The distraction had given Randall time to think too. He fixed his eyes on her and went for the jugular. 'We have reason to believe,' he said, 'that the person you buried and claimed the life insurance for following the sailing accident was not, in fact, your husband, but his friend, Mr Poulson.'

He was leaving out any accusations of infidelity – for the moment.

Verity's eyes flickered, disturbance in their ocean-blue depths. Her mouth opened and quickly closed as though to supress anything that might have slipped out. It wasn't much of a sign but to the two watching officers it looked very much like panic.

'What on earth makes you think that?' Her voice was only slightly less controlled, a little more harsh. She blinked.

'A man was murdered recently in Shrewsbury, Shropshire,' Randall said. 'We have reason to believe that he is or was your husband.'

Verity frowned. It wasn't marked by much movement in her forehead – Botox, Randall guessed.

'This man was a vagrant.'

Verity laughed. 'You're trying to tell me that Simeon was a vagrant? Why?' She threw her arms out in an all-encompassing, expansive movement. 'Why on earth would he do that when if he really was alive he would own this place and a huge flourishing factory?'

'From the information he gave in his note-book it would appear following the sailing tragedy he became disillusioned with life.' Randall was choosing his words and phrases very carefully, delicately avoiding implicating Verity van Helsing in her husband's attempted murder and in the actual crime of a few weeks ago.

Verity leaned back in her chair, her face, under the make-up, pale.

'We believe the Van Helsing Shoe Company,' Randall continued smoothly, 'was not proving quite the success that previous generations of the family had achieved.'

Verity seized on this aspect. Her one familiar point of reference. 'That's true,' she said sharply. 'If Simeon had lived . . .' She blinked a few times in rapid succession, as though blinking away threatened tears. But Randall was not deceived. 'We found a child's shoe stitched into his coat.'

Verity looked startled. But she hadn't finished fighting yet. 'If Simeon had lived the business would have stagnated – not moved forward into the area which has proved so successful.'

'Shoes for the Stars,' Randall said, quoting one of the selling points on her website.

In spite of the seriousness of her position and the pending accusation, Verity looked pleased with herself – almost smug, as though she had forgotten why they were there. 'Yes,' she agreed.

Randall leaned forward for the kill. 'It must have been quite a shock to you to discover that you husband was living the life of a hobo in Shropshire.'

She blinked.

Randall fixed his eyes on her. 'Who was it who recognized him?'

She licked her lips, took a sip of tea, undecided how to proceed.

'We have a description of this man,' Randall said. He'd dropped all pretence of conciliation now. 'Who was it?'

She couldn't speak.

Randall took the opportunity to press his point home. Dagger, sword, rapier thrust. Lunge. 'Look,' he said. 'It's possible, in the absence of

233

proof, that there will be no charge made against you.' He watched as her eyes narrowed and she started to work it all out.

'But your husband *was* murdered and we think you know who did it. Someone recognized him on the streets of Shrewsbury and, just in case he surfaced again, possibly testified against you and your dead lover who was, incidentally, also your co-conspirator, he killed him.'

Finally she burst. 'Simeon was letting the business go down the chute.' To her, this was justification.

Randall ignored the remark or the rising animosity he felt against this woman. 'Your co-conspirator,' he continued, hardly pausing, 'Rafael Poulson, who is, incidentally, buried under your husband's name after you wrongly identified him.'

'Cremated, actually.' It gave her pleasure to score even this one small point over him.

Randall shrugged, glanced at Talith whose face, initially impassive, was now looking at Verity van Helsing not with admiration but more with something like revulsion. As you would look at a beautiful but deadly snake.

'You deliberately misidentified Rafael Poulson as your husband so you could claim life insurance.'

'I was upset,' she said. 'Traumatized by the accident.' She'd clearly already practised that line. It came out so pat.

'And a few weeks ago someone did murder your husband,' Randall said. 'They cut his throat and left him. Who was it?'

And the room suddenly fell quiet and still as though the three people in it were part of a tableaux. Randall had said what he'd come to say. Talith had kept silent, merely observing events with increasing distaste. And Verity? She didn't yet know to play it.

Randall waited.

Thirty-Two

They gave her five minutes, during which they watched various emotions swim across her face. Anxiety, worry, uncertainty, and finally a decision. She stood up.

'Would you like to have a look around my factory?'

It was a cue. Both officers stood up too.

'If you don't mind,' she said, confidence now absent from her tone, 'I'd rather travel in my own car . . .' There was a hint of a smile. 'Less conspicuous.'

As they left the house they heard her say, very softly, to herself, 'I always wondered who took the shoe.'

Randall nodded.

As expected, the factory was smart, ostentatious, sitting like a queen in beautifully landscaped grounds and a directors' car park full of Lexuses, Mercs and Jaguars.

Verity drew in a deep breath as the doors opened and a tall brunette rose from behind the desk and greeted her. 'Morning, Mrs Van Helsing. We wondered what time you'd be in.'

Then her eyes moved to the two detectives and they watched as she took this in. Without comment she sat back down in her seat, her eyes moving between the detectives and her CEO.

Wisely, she said nothing. They glanced around

the hallway lined with photographs of the Van Helsing dynasty. And there was their man. Intelligent but not too sure of himself, trying to exude confidence and competence but not quite managing either. Randall stepped forward to look closer at his face, taking in the carefully crossed hands, the benign expression, benevolent, father-like, the lack of arrogance. He would have been a good employer but not necessarily a good businessman.

In the centre of the reception area stood a glass case with the story of the little girl who had eventually become Simeon van Helsing's grand-mother typed out alongside just one shoe. There was a darker area on the silk where the second shoe had once stood and was now in a police evidence bag in Shrewsbury.

Verity van Helsing rapped out a question to the startled girl. 'Is Hiram in?'

The girl nodded. 'He's in . . . his office.' Her voice had slowed as she patently wondered what the hell was going on.

Verity walked slowly along a corridor, passing doors. Each door had a name on it. She passed her own door with Verity van Helsing, CEO on it and her footsteps slowed as she reached a door beyond with the name Hiram Schumacher, Deputy CEO. She knocked just once, opened the door and stood back.

Schumacher fitted the bill: tall, stocky, blonde, in his forties. Initially glad to see Verity, he was not so pleased when Randall and Talith stepped forward.

He was, at first, arrogantly blustering. 'What

on earth's going on?' He appealed to his boss. 'Verity?'

She simply regarded him without expression, without emotion, as though she was a blank canvas. There was no accusation, no recrimination. Nothing. Nothing between these two people except a sort of sorrow.

'Mr Schumacher,' Randall said. He did not want to arrest him at this point. They had absolutely no hard evidence – yet. 'Would you mind coming to Shrewsbury Police Station?' He gave a bland smile. 'To help us with our enquiries.'

Thirty-Three

It was two days later that Randall again visited Martha to give her an update on the case. She knew instantly that events had gone well.

'Well,' he said, 'luckily for us, Schumacher, which incidentally sounds very much like a German shoemaker, is a careless man, or should I say cocky? Or should I just say he really didn't expect to be found out. He was completely shocked when we knocked on his door at Van Helsing's Shoes. Who on earth would connect the apparently random murder of a tramp with him? Wealthy, successful and without a criminal record. But luckily for us he hadn't cleaned his car properly; neither, rather stupidly, had he destroyed the clothes he was wearing that night and, believe it or not, we even have the knife – the murder weapon, back in its block in his kitchen. Twice through the dishwasher doesn't quite remove all traces of blood. Any one of those pieces of forensic evidence would have been enough to proverbially hang him.'

'So you have a case.'

He nodded.

'What was he doing up here in Shrewsbury?'

Randall looked smug. 'Believe it or not, he was looking into shooting some advertising here. He was looking at various locations including . . .'

239

'Moreton Corbet,' Martha supplied. 'So what did he do? Discover our man at the ruin?'

Randall shook his head. 'No,' he said. 'He followed him out of Shrewsbury. He'd already seen where he hung out, even the work he did for Miss Dreyfuss. He watched him in the fields and when the time came simply followed him out of Shrewsbury, waiting for his opportunity. When Van Helsing was picked up by the lorry Schumacher simply followed the vehicle until it dropped him off at Moreton Corbet. Then Schumacher went after him. Once Simeon had gone down into the cellar he – well. You know the rest.'

'I don't know why,' she said. 'Why would he risk it?'

'He believed the factory would fold if events came to light.'

'How so?'

Randall drew in a deep breath. 'Look at it this way, Martha. Under Van Helsing the factory had a shaky ride. It almost came close to going under. Part recession, but really our tramp wasn't a visionary like his wife; neither was he a great businessman. He'd existed with machinery that was outdated. And he certainly wouldn't have had the genius to organize the Shoes for the Stars campaign. Besides . . .' Randall was staring out of the window at the town, '. . . there was the question of money and the attempted murder. Verity would very likely have ended up in jail whatever her story about memory loss and confusion. And all the negative publicty that would be generated around the firm . . .' He paused. 'As

Schumacher put it, he was sacrificing a sprat to preserve a mackerel.'

Martha blinked. 'To cut his throat.'

'Yes,' Randall said. 'An extraordinary thing. He seemed to think it would endear me to him when he said that he really hadn't enjoyed doing that but he'd wanted to be sure that Van Helsing really was dead this time around. He'd read about another tramp being murdered and thought the police – us, of course – would be sure to think it was just gangland violence.' Randall paused. 'He didn't say this and I don't have proof, but I'm pretty sure part of his plan was to blackmail Verity.'

'For money?'

'Maybe for money, but possibly he'd force her to marry him – blackmail.'

'Oh.' She eyed him. 'It wouldn't exactly make for a very happy marriage, would it?'

Randall shook his head.

'There is one thing puzzling me,' Martha said. 'How did Schumacher recognize him? The two hadn't worked together, had they? Simeon van Helsing clearly says in his account that he didn't know him.'

Of course, Randall thought. *Martha hadn't been there, had she; she hadn't been to the factory.*

'Portraits,' Randall explained. 'They hang all the way around the reception area. Schumacher must have looked at them every day he walked in; the family is practically a legend.'

'You have a strong case?'

Randall nodded. 'He's confessed.'

'So he goes to jail, whereas Verity gets off scot-free?'

'We're going to get nowhere if we go after her. There simply isn't any evidence and she'll just say that she was in a distraught state when she misidentified her husband. A jury would buy that and she would invite sympathy. After all, she wasn't the killer, though I suspect that Schumacher told her he'd seen her husband and I'm pretty sure he would have told her that he'd got rid of him. I wouldn't be at all surprised if she even went to Moreton Corbet to see the scene of the crime. It's even possible . . .' Randall knew he was being fanciful here, 'that she laid some of the flowers that we saw on his grave.'

Martha was thoughtful, then said, 'So now I can re-open the inquest and we have an exhumation and a reburial?'

Again Randall nodded but he looked on his guard. 'What are you up to, Martha?' he asked warily.

Thirty-Four

After the initial slow process, events now moved fast.

The stone was discreetly removed from Rafael Poulson's burial site and a cross with his name on it erected instead. There was nothing to exhume as he'd been cremated. The man had drowned accidentally when the boat had capsized. Hunter had become the hunted, the killer the victim. It hadn't been exactly what he and Verity had planned, but that was how he had died and she had cleverly worked around the change in circumstances. Events had been deliberately made hazy by the survivors of the sordid little affair. Simeon van Helsing's remains were exhumed from his anonymous grave and reburied with full honours, but Martha still felt there was unfinished business.

Verity van Helsing had got off scot-free, which seemed wrong to her. If anything the woman had profited richly from her scheme. Whatever her ultimate goal – and Verity was a woman whose mind was as devious as Hampton Court Maze – she had played her part in her lover's death as well as her husband's departure from his life. And Martha was convinced that she had had something to do with her husband's murder. Indirectly, obscurely, she was responsible. The trouble would be proving it. Hiram Schumacher was remaining silent over Verity's part in the death at Moreton Corbet. But Martha knew instinctively that this woman was at the not only centre of the tragedies but the cause of them. A modern Lady Macbeth.

But she had to be very careful, tread a fine line. There were rigid rules and regulations about inquests and the role of the coroner, and finger pointing at an accused was definitely not part of the procedure.

She rang the coroner whose jurisdiction covered West Sussex, the area where the sailing tragedy had taken place, and spent a while explaining what had happened subsequently and her involvement in the case. He agreed to allow her to conduct the inquest on Rafael Poulson at the same time as that of Simeon van Helsing. Now this gave her a little more scope for her own scheme.

She told Alex a little of her intention and he raised his eyebrows and looked vaguely concerned. 'You sure this is a good idea?'

She thought carefully before answering. 'No,' she said steadily, 'it isn't a good idea. But that isn't the point. I want justice for our wandering tramp.' She met his eyes boldly. 'That's what it's about, Alex – justice.'

He nodded and shifted uncomfortably in his chair. He was frowning, his long legs restless. Finally he got up and left.

And so her court was reconvened late in November and she met Verity van Helsing for the first time face-to-face, summoned as a witness. Martha

244

wasn't surprised to feel instant revulsion for the woman.

The press were there, taking notes, curious about the breaking story, scenting blood. As she took her seat, Martha reflected on recent events. Simeon had been quietly reburied with dignity in Shrewsbury and Genevieve Dreyfuss, Martha knew, visited the grave often and laid flowers on it. Martha knew she did this out of a sense of misguided guilt, but at least he had someone to mourn him.

She also knew that the insurance company who had paid up the hefty sum on Simeon's life (and whose idea had that been? Martha wondered) were 'having talks' with Verity. Whether it would lead to a criminal conviction for fraud Martha didn't know, but she understood that there would be a fine for false information and possibly the life insurance money would have to be repaid. Perhaps that should suffice. But it wouldn't be enough for her. She wanted more.

Not surprisingly, when Jericho had contacted Mrs Van Helsing to summon her to court she had demurred. The publicity would, she had said, damage her business and was it really necessary as she had nothing to contribute with regards to her husband's murder. Jericho, under instruction from Martha, had insisted, hinting that she could be subpoenaed to appear if necessary. And that, he had said, adding this little bit off his own bat, might provoke even more interest and adverse publicity.

'Surely,' he'd said cleverly, 'you'd want to be

at the inquest of your husband and his . . . close friend?'

She'd had no answer to that.

Well then, Martha thought, if that's the best we can do, so be it. Let's damage your business, widow Van Helsing.

27 November was a Thursday and dawned bright and cold. Martha donned a navy suit – sometimes one had to get out of black. Underneath the jacket she wore a white silk blouse and finished it all with high-heeled navy shoes, the sort you could walk in. She felt she should dress up for Simeon van Helsing's day in court.

Martha had planned very carefully what to say.

She scanned the room. The pathologist from West Sussex was present – she'd spoken to him again at length. As she was a doctor they had quickly established a rapport and, when she had given him the backstory, he had been intrigued enough to travel up to Shropshire.

She began, as usual, with her opening speech.

'You may find it very strange, ladies and gentlemen, that the inquests on Simeon van Helsing, the man who was a vagrant in the environs of Shrewsbury and who was murdered in September in the grounds of Moreton Corbet Castle, and Rafael Poulson, who drowned in a sailing accident in West Sussex five years ago, should both be held here, in Shrewsbury. Be patient . . .' She scanned the room. 'There is a connection.'

She paused. 'I shall relate events chronologically and perhaps all will be made clear.' She glanced down at her notes. 'March the fifth, in the year 2000, was a Sunday. It was cold and blustery. Nevertheless, three people, a husband, wife and male friend, decided to go sailing in a boat called . . .' She couldn't resist a glance at Randall, who was watching her with a fascinated, rapt look tinged with apprehension, 'the *Lucy Manette*.'

Alex gave a nod, understanding, and she carried on. 'The exact circumstances of the tragedy are unclear. What is certain is that the boat capsized. One person, a man, was later found drowned and identified as her husband by Verity van Helsing, who survived the accident.' Here she allowed her eyes to dwell, just for a moment, on Verity van Helsing, who was wearing an expensive-looking black suit, and a hat with a veil which hid her eyes and her face, except for a pink-lipsticked mouth.

'The man was subsequently buried as Simeon van Helsing and the million-pound life insurance money was paid out. The other body was never found.' She waited. The court was silent, knowing there was more – much more.

'Only one person knows what happened that day on the *Lucy Manette* – Mrs Van Helsing.' She addressed the woman directly. 'I know you've already given an account of the tragedy to the West Sussex coroner. But we now know that the man whom *you* . . .' she dropped the emphasis to sit, heavy and accusatory, in the courtroom like a bad smell, 'identified as your husband, apparently drowned, in fact was not your husband but your . . . *family friend*.' Again,

247

she allowed the phase to be suggestive. 'Perhaps . . .' Martha directed a sugary sweet smile at Verity. 'Perhaps you'd like to give us the *true* account of that Sunday in March?' She tried to ignore the furious look Verity van Helsing aimed at her, but was delighted to see the gentlemen of the press were taking copious notes. Now what, she wondered, would be their headlines? *Widow in tragic mix up*? Or something else? Something a little less innocent, a little more pointed. A little more perceptive and subtly accusatory? Would they be taken in by Verity's pretty face and slight figure or would they see right through to her other side? *The dark side.* Would any of them dare to make the connection between one fatal accident and a murder, look at the common denominator and, oh, yes, point a finger at the innocent-looking and beautiful Mrs Van Helsing? A bit of trial by headline?

Verity made her elegant way towards the witness box and turned towards Martha, as though ready to challenge her. Instead she said softly and politely. 'Where do you want me to start, Coroner?'

'First of all,' Martha said, 'would you like to tell me who the man who died in the boating accident five years ago *really* was?'

Had Verity been a cat she would have hissed and had her claws out by now instead of simply tightening her lips. 'It seems as if he must have been Mr Poulson.'

Martha was determined to hammer this one out – hard. 'And remind me – who,' she asked, eyes wide, '*was* Mr Poulson?'

'Mr Rafael Poulson was a close friend of my

husband's.' Verity couldn't quite conceal her irritation.

Martha sometimes wished she wore glasses. It would have given her account some natural pauses as she took them on and off. Time to think. 'We have here a letter . . .' she scanned the room, 'verified as having been written by your husband, Mr Simeon van Helsing, which puts a rather different light on that.'

Verity licked her lips. 'Letter?'

The rules of disclosure did not apply to coroner's courts, unlike courts of law.

'Yes,' Martha said. And if Verity was struggling not to sound guilty *she* was making a similar effort not to sound smug. 'It was left by Mr Simeon van Helsing, concealed near the place where he was murdered. This letter gives us a different account of the relationship between Mr Poulson and your husband which appears to give us another story.' She held the transcript up. 'I quote: *"We had many friends, amongst whom was a man called Rafael Poulson. I don't know how he became one of our circle of friends. He liked boats and said he'd been in the military like his father and grandfather before him. Another family business, he joked. I didn't even think Verity liked him. But perhaps dancers can be actresses too. I never saw her speak to him but he was apparently one of our friends. Suddenly there he was."'*

Martha paused to allow the words and their tacit implication time to sink in then she addressed the court again. 'However, the purpose of this court is not to investigate the origins of

249

friendships but to ascertain who died, where, when and, if possible, why or how.' She knew the law demanded she stop there. If the CPS found the letter inadmissible as evidence and not enough to charge the widow then she would be in contempt of court if she carried on – however tempted she might be.

She turned again to the widow. 'So, Mrs Van Helsing, you were in the boat with this mutual friend, and the boat capsized.' She scanned the room. Everyone was watching. There was an air of tension. Verity was watching her very warily, anxiety marking her face even with the paralysing effect of Botox.

She responded in a breathy, Marilyn Monroe sort of voice. 'That's correct. I don't remember exactly what happened or how. I just remember the boat going over with a huge, horrible splash.' She put a tissue to her eyes as though to blot tears. But Martha was near enough to see that there were none.

'I believe you managed to secure yourself to a life raft.'

Verity nodded. 'I hardly remember,' she said. 'I suppose I must have done. And then I was rescued.'

Martha could feel a subtle change wash over the court. Verity was doing a great acting job but it wasn't winning her any sympathy from the courtroom.

She moved on briskly. 'Quite. And then what, Mrs Van Helsing?'

'I was called in on the following day to identify my husband.'

'Aah.' Martha held her finger up to make sure everyone heard, particularly the members of the press who would, if they wanted, make much of this. 'Your husband.'

And now the widow looked distinctly wary. She was worried what Martha was about to say.

'I have a found a little out about Mr Poulson. He was six feet tall, was he not?'

'I – I don't know. I don't remember.' She looked around the courtroom desperately, searching for a friendly face. 'It was a long time ago. I was traumatized.'

'Whereas your husband's height was five feet nine inches.'

Again, she stopped while Verity watched her, wide-eyed with apprehension.

Martha ploughed on doggedly. 'Mr Poulson was also balding whereas your husband had a full head of hair, did he not?'

'I didn't look that closely. I was in such a state.'

Martha felt the ripple go around the room with a sense of satisfaction. Gotcha.

'I was very upset,' Verity continued, still trying to convince the court, whereas she didn't need to. 'I was in shock,' she insisted, unaware that Martha had no jurisdiction over wrongful identification.

'Nevertheless,' Martha continued smoothly, 'whatever the circumstances, it would appear that the man buried as your husband was, in fact, Rafael Poulson.' She looked around the room with the blandest of expression. 'Family

251

friend. It would *appear* a case of wrongful identity.'

Verity fidgeted, itching to get out of that witness stand. But Martha hadn't quite finished with her yet.

To prolong the agony she summoned the pathologist who had performed the post-mortem on Rafael Poulson and asked him to detail the man's injuries and cause of death.

Pathologists were frequently quite defensive when such a mistake had occurred, but in this case he was a competent, experienced pathologist with probably only a year or two to go before retiring. He was perfectly comfortable giving evidence under such circumstances.

'The primary cause of death,' he said, 'was drowning. Sea water was expelled from the lungs during the procedure. A contributory factor would have been a nasty blow on the head, possibly from the boom swinging across at the time when the boat capsized. The gentleman had been in the water some hours so hypothermia might also have played a part in his inability to keep afloat or, indeed, to make his way to the life raft, which had been inflated.'

Martha pursed her lips and sneaked a glance at Verity, who looked pale but defiant. She wondered then. Had Verity tried to get Poulson into the life raft or not? They would probably never know.

She addressed the pathologist again. 'There was no suspicion of foul play on Mr Poulson's body?'

The pathologist paused. He knew exactly what

she was getting at. 'The man wrongly identified as Mr Simeon van Helsing and now identified as being Rafael Poulson had injuries and a cause of death consistent with drowning in sea water following a sailing mishap.' He met Martha's eyes. 'There was nothing to either prove or disprove foul play.'

He raised his eyebrows. A mute, but unmistakable message. *You won't push me further than that, Coroner Gunn.*

She bowed her head, acknowledging his experience and professionalism. 'In that case, I have to concur with my West Sussex colleague that the cause of death of the man brought from the sea on 7 March 2000 wrongly identified as Simeon van Helsing and now known to be Rafael Poulson was drowning, and therefore my verdict is one of misadventure.' She eyed the press. 'In other words, I have to concur with the pathologist. This appears an accident.'

Like obedient schoolkids, they duly scribbled.

'Now then, back to the real Simeon van Helsing, who was still very much alive. Mrs Van Helsing, can you think of any reason why your husband did not return home when he had survived the boating accident?'

Zombie-like, Verity shook her head.

'And why he made the unusual choice to adopt the life of a vagrant?'

Another mute shake of the head and a dab of the eye.

She let her go.

Martha then addressed the court. 'Mr Van

253

Helsing offered some explanation in a letter he wrote. He hid this account in the castle where his body was found. I understand the police are considering it as evidence.' She would love to have been able to then say, *and on the strength of it, considering prosecution*, but she sensed Alex Randall's shoulders stiffening and knew she could go so far and no further.

'However, as far as the gentleman we now know to be Simeon van Helsing is concerned, we shall hear first from the pathologist. Doctor Sullivan?'

Mark duly rose and approached the witness box, swore on oath and looked across at her. 'Would you give us your findings, please?'

'The body we now know to be that of Mr Simeon van Helsing was found at Moreton Corbet Castle on September the twelfth at ten-thirty a.m. I pronounced him dead at the scene and estimated that he had died some time the previous evening, probably about eighteen hours earlier. The body was removed to the mortuary in Shrewsbury and I performed a post-mortem at nine a.m. on Monday, September the fifteenth.'

There followed a list of people present at the post-mortem, details of procedure and samples taken.

Martha sneaked a glance at Verity. She looked pale and was swaying very slightly. She sent a coded message to Jericho. He handed her a glass of water.

'The cause of death, Doctor Sullivan?'

'The cause of death of Mr Van Helsing,' Mark

said heavily, 'was shock due to haemorrhage due to a fatal throat wound.'

'Was it possible he could have inflicted this wound on himself?'

A slow shake of the head. 'And no weapon was found nearby.'

He gave out a few more details, a low alcohol level, no contributory factors of disease. Martha risked another look at Verity, who had now pulled her veil right down over her face. 'So, Doctor Sullivan, you agree that Mr Simeon van Helsing's death was due to homicide.' Again, she addressed the wider court in a loud, clear voice. 'I understand the police have made an arrest.' Another pause to give her next statement clear emphasis. 'I understand the person charged with Mr Van Helsing's murder is a colleague of yours, Mrs Van Helsing.'

No response from the bench.

Martha would have loved to have made a sarcastic comment about two of her friends being touched by tragedy, but she didn't dare. All she could do was steer the press towards an observation.

She continued, 'In fact, an employee of Van Helsing Shoe Company.' She had been determined to mention the firm.

Another pause.

'And I understand that the perpetrator is a man who I believe to have been very loyal towards you and your company, someone who only joined the firm four years ago, after your husband's disappearance.'

Verity lifted her veil just long enough to shoot

Martha a fiery stare. Then she dropped the black lace over her face again.

The verdicts were a foregone conclusion, that Poulson had died as a result of an accident and Simeon's was homicide. Martha didn't need to add, by person or persons unknown.

Thirty-Five

Monday, 22 December, midday.

It was almost a month later that Alex called in
her office. Christmas was looming, Sukey was
home for the holiday and Sam was preparing for
the Boxing Day match. Jericho had erected a
small Christmas tree in the lobby. Martha had
read the headlines after the inquest and knew
that, as anticipated, no charge had been made
against Verity van Helsing. She did have some
consolation, though. Shares in the Van Helsing
Shoe Company had dropped with the news that
the USA, Australia and France had cancelled their
military contracts. The scandal had had a knock-
on effect.

A few celebrities were also reputed to have
pulled out, citing a discomfort with the adverse
publicity of the two cases which were intertwined
as fatally as bindweed to the Van Helsing Shoe
Company. Martha felt that, to some extent, the
man they had dubbed 'Charles' had had his
revenge. But how cold a dish.

She wasn't sure she would ever really understand his motives for dropping out so completely
from his previous privileged life. Why hadn't he
simply gone to the police and told them what he
knew? Could it possibly have been because he'd
known the business he'd inherited would finally

257

fold? Had his best contribution for Van Helsing Shoes been to disappear, to vaporize? Had he still felt a misguided love for his treacherous wife? Who could know?

Something else bothered her – another point that she would never have answered. Simeon van Helsing had hidden his books in the chimney, both the novel and the exercise book. Why then? Had he then known that the man who had seen him in the town was stalking him like a tiger through the jungle? Had he foreseen his destiny?

And while she understood him carrying the little girl's clog around with him, a simple reminder of the best of human nature, had he really carried the Second World War medals around to remind him of the opposite? Of treachery, perjury and lies?

What she didn't know and what was disturbing her was how DI Alex Randall had viewed her performance at the inquest. He hadn't been in touch since then and that made her uneasy. So she was glad when he rang on that Monday afternoon, giving no clue as to his view, simply asking, in a terse voice, whether he could come and see her in her office.

'Of course, Alex,' she said, and waited uneasily for his arrival.

She had time to reflect. When one was young and sure of one's attractiveness to the opposite sex things were so much simpler. Now, looking back, she had taken so much for granted. But now – oh, it was so easy to fall into big mistakes, bigger misunderstandings and a state of toe-curling embarrassment by misreading the signs.

She needn't have worried. When he arrived he was wearing a large grin, a pair of smart navy jeans and a pale blue sweater. He walked in with a confidence she hadn't seen before.

'Martha,' he said. 'Sorry I haven't been in touch. We've been finalising the case against Mr Schumacher, who paints an interesting story.'

'Go on.'

There was a twinkle in his eye as he continued. 'Let's go somewhere for lunch. My Christmas treat. Somewhere nice.'

So they found themselves in the lovely panelled room of Drapers' Hall. Right in the middle of town, in St Mary's Square, opposite the church, studying the menu. 'This is nice, Alex,' she said impulsively.

'Go on, say it,' he said. 'We should do it more often.'

She should have said then, *Woah*, held her hands up and made her intentions clear – or at least clearer. But she didn't and this omission would have long shadows which would one day reach into the most private corner of her life.

'Well,' Alex continued, perfectly at ease, 'our Mr Schumacher has come completely clean and told us everything – and more. He claims he was having an affair with Verity who, incidentally, completely denies all this, but he will have his say in court, Martha. He won't go down for murder without a struggle.'

'Good.'

'He told us that the beautiful Verity . . .'

So you had noticed.

DI Randall continued smoothly, oblivious to

her wince, '. . . had promised to marry him.' He made a face, 'Though I doubt it somehow. Blackmailed into marrying him, more like. Anyway, it would have been impossible had her husband still been alive. The life insurance and assets would have been strained. And besides . . . he knew full well that the scandal would destroy the company. Their reputation had been built up on a fourth-generation family business: traditional, personal care, everything ethical and above board caring for their customers' generations and so on. The tragedy of Simeon's presumed drowning only enhanced the sense of a personal, family business. Since the news of the mix up, his strange decision to become wilfully homeless and the murder broke, their shares have plummeted. One whiff of scandal and many of their customers have abandoned them.'

'I know,' she said, spooning some mashed potato into her mouth.

There was an answering light in Randall's eyes. 'I guessed you would. Martha,' he said tentatively. And stopped.

And she didn't know whether she wanted him to finish the sentence or not. She didn't know what to say, whether to stop him right there, when she didn't know what it was he had been about to say. She eyed him then put her fork down and waited.

Alex Randall gave a deep, drawn-out sigh, smiled, reached out and touched her hand. 'Oh, Martha,' he said.

'Good gracious.' The voice came from over her shoulder. 'Martha. Darling. Wonderful to see you.

260

I'm so sorry I haven't been in touch. I've been abroad. Expanding the business, you know, to the Cayman Islands.'

She stood up, flustered. Simon Pendlebury. Of all the rotten luck. Alex Randall seemed to shrink beside the confident and charismatic Simon Pendlebury, he of extortionate wealth and a widower, parent of two of the nastiest young women she'd ever met. Pendlebury bent and kissed her cheek.

She introduced the two men and felt their wariness and suspicion, skirting around each other like two wrestlers, shaking hands almost with their fists closed.

She looked beyond Simon and sighted a young woman in a very tight black skirt and some impressive high heels. 'My new secretary,' he said, wafting a careless hand. 'Cerys Watkins.'

She was a stunning-looking woman – confident, too. Long, thick, straight black hair which fell to her waist, a pale, flawless complexion, startling blue eyes and scarlet lipstick.

She held out her hand. 'I can't believe my luck,' she said in an undisguised Welsh accent. 'I've heard such a lot about you from Simon. I've been dyin' to meet you.'

Martha simply smiled. Truth was she warmed to Cerys immediately. Her accent reminded her of her gentle, tolerant father smoking his pipe in the greenhouse.

'They all love you, you know, Hannah, Jocasta, Armenia. They all think the world of you.'

So . . . Simon's housekeeper and his two daughters. That was nice.

261

Cerys turned her attention to Alex Randall, who was standing back, maybe in the hope that they would not notice him or maybe it was simple embarrassment.

'And you are?'

Alex Randall held his hand out with a warm smile at Cerys and her boss.

'Detective Inspector Alex Randall,' he said without embarrassment. 'Martha and I were sort of celebrating, sort of discussing a recent case we've both been involved in.

'Oh,' Cerys said. 'That's nice.'

They all shook hands. Simon suggested they share a coffee in the bar area and the four of them sat down, drinking, enjoying each other's company.

It could almost be, Martha thought, two couples. A foursome.

But it's never going to be, Martha, said the annoying, honest voice deep inside her. *DI Alex Randall, for all his friendliness towards you, is a married man.*

But his words pushed insistently into her brain. *I wish she would die.*

That one phrase made her nervous for the future.